HOW TO DATE YOUR DRAGON

MOLLY HARPER

COPYRIGHT

How to Date Your Dragon

ISBN: 978-1-64197-049-5

This ebook is based on an Audible Original audiobook.

NYLA Publishing
121 W 27th St., Suite 1201, New York, NY 10001
http://www.nyliterary.com

ACKNOWLEDGMENTS

I am so very grateful for the series of fortunate events that led to this project. My endless appreciation, as ever, to Natanya Wheeler, who created this opportunity from thin air. Thanks go to Rose Hilliard, she of the infinite enthusiasm and author of the gentlest editorial letters ever – who didn't even flinch when I asked, "What if we use ALL the shifters ... and some creatures people haven't even heard of?" And thanks to author Jaye Wells, who helped me come up with a better name for the series than, "That Audio Series I Can't Seem to Come Up With a Good Name For." And thank you to Louisiana State University and Cajunradio.org, for the online resources they have provided regarding Cajun French phrases and pronunciations. And as always, thank you to my family, who support me through my writing benders with chocolate and bottomless cups of tea.

1

JILLIAN

Jillian Ramsay, PhD, was driving a panel van without air-conditioning through an area known as the Devil's Armpit.

She wished that was an exaggeration, or a misprint on the map. But there it was, in bold print on the highway sign, "You are entering the Devil's Armpit."

She supposed she should be thankful that her destination wasn't the Devil's Armpit, an unusually sulfurous section of southern Louisiana that smelled of rotten eggs and damnation, but a small town just beyond it—Mystic Bayou. She hoped the more attractive name also indicated a more appealing odor. Dr. Montes hadn't left anything in his field notes about bringing air fresheners with him. But then again, she'd come to learn Dr. Montes's methods were less polished than anyone hoped.

Jillian fanned her face and dabbed at the perspiration dotting her upper lip. The air-conditioning had crapped out within fifteen minutes of her leaving the New Orleans airport, but after a flight from Chile involving two layovers and a lengthy argument with customs over her audio-video equipment, she just didn't have any fight left in her.

She rolled down the window, just a crack, hoping the muggy late May air would be cooler than the interior of the van. Almost immediately, her nostrils were flooded with the smell of what could only be described as Satan's BO.

"Mistake! Huge error in judgment!" she gasped.

Jillian rolled up the window, her hands so sweaty that her fingers actually slipped off of the handle a few times before she sealed herself inside the van. Eager for some form of odor-free distraction, she used her hands-free dialer to call Sonja Fong at the League office. She grumbled as the call went to voicemail, *again*. But when the machine went *beep,* Jillian tried to make her tone more suited for a friend she was actually fond of, as opposed to a telemarketer.

"Hey, Sonja, it's me again. I'd really appreciate a call back, so maybe you could explain to me what's really going on back there. The League keeps assuring me that everything's just fine, as they turn my life completely upside down. But I keep getting the feeling I'm a heroine in one of those awful seventies horror movies, where the unwitting outsider ends up a human sacrifice. Cell phone reception is getting pretty spotty, so if you can, call back soon. Love you, bye."

Jillian pursed her lips. This was not a very auspicious beginning to her first real field assignment. She'd flown all the way to Santiago, only to get a call that her mentor and boss had been seriously injured on his assignment in northern England, and the International League for Interspecies Cooperation was sending her in his place to southern Louisiana. Her in-depth study of the *mohana* and their mating habits would just have to wait.

All that background reading on malevolent sex-obsessed dolphin shapeshifters for nothing.

Nearly an hour later, Jillian had sweated completely through her clothes and was beginning to worry that she was lost. The gnarled trees dripping with Spanish moss were all starting to look the same. She was pretty sure she'd passed a carnation-pink shack on stilts twice, and she'd realized those "logs" resting against the banks of the swamp, dangerously close to the road, had legs and very large jaws. She was beyond jet-lagged, couldn't remember her last application of deodorant and was starting to think maybe the League could go jump into the murky, gator-filled water looming on either side of the highway.

Just as Jillian started to search for a place to either do a three-point turn or sleep for the night, another sign came into view. It read, *Welcome to Mystic Bayou, Home of the Fighting Marsh Dogs*, over a caricature of a large rat with its fists raised *a la* the Fighting Irish.

Jillian nodded. "OK, then."

Maybe it was better for her to stay lost.

Jillian opened the van window again, hoping that maybe the air in Mystic Bayou was more palatable. She took a tentative breath. She could almost taste the sweetness on the air, redolent with honeysuckle and dried grass and earth. She took several gulps of it, lifting her mass of honey blond hair off her sweaty neck. She balked at the reflection in the rearview mirror, wondering who let that pale, sweaty woman with the under-eye luggage into the driver's seat.

She was due to meet her community liaison in just a few minutes and she was a mess. Maybe she could duck into the back of the van to freshen up before she met Mayor Berend? That was something legitimate scientists did, right? Change their clothes in vans?

The town quickly came into view in that "suddenly there are buildings and if you blink you will miss them all" way unique to tiny rural towns. Main Street was pretty much the only street from what Jillian could see, with the occasional short side street branching out into clusters of two to three small homes. Dr. Montes had written that few families lived in town, preferring to keep almost clannish compounds in the outlying areas of the county and only venturing into town limits for errands.

Main Street led to a town square centered on a gazebo, and, behind that, a large white-washed building topped with a golden shape she couldn't quite make out. The street boasted a freshly painted collection of businesses with flower baskets hanging from every surface, giving the town a cheerful, neatly kept air. Aside from the inordinate number of them that seemed to involve taxidermy, there was a bank, a boat dealership, a grocery, an "apothecary," a beauty salon, a book shop, a newspaper called the Mystic Messenger, and finally, Bathtilda's Pie Shop, which boasted the world's best chocolate rhubarb pie. Jillian had never heard of chocolate rhubarb pie, but frankly it sounded a bit gross. Each business had a little addition under the shop name stating, "Owned and Operated by Bonner Boone" or "Owned and Operated by Branwyn Boone," or in the sweet shop's case, "Bathtilda Boone." Was every business in town owned by a Boone?

Dr. Montes's instructions were to go to City Hall, which appeared to be the tall, white building at the end of the street. With a gold spire rising from a bell tower-like structure on the roof, it was the tallest building in town. As she drove closer, she spotted a gold-and-green SUV marked "Sheriff" parked out front, next to a rather large Harley Davidson with custom-painted claw marks raking down the body.

She parked the cursed van in an empty spot, near the fountain that stood across from Mystic Bayou City Hall's door. She glanced down the street at the sweet shop and wondered if she could duck in unnoticed and change clothes in the restroom. It would probably cause a bit of a stir. She couldn't imagine a town like this got a lot of tourists hauling luggage into public restrooms with them. But it would be better than—

Jillian shrieked. "What the hell!"

A huge man in an extremely tight black t-shirt and even

tighter jeans was staring at her through her driver side window. He stood several inches taller than the van, and his hands were the size of picnic hams. He had thick, wildly curling black hair tied back in a ponytail and a matching beard that spread across his barrel chest. His smoke gray eyes seemed to penetrate through the window glass, making her shiver despite the muggy heat.

He raised a hand, and it was all she could do not to flinch. "Hi, there."

A friendly grin spread across his face, warming his features as he waggled a massive hand.

Should she roll down the window? Was it safe? At this point, it would be rude not to, but she'd always read that a woman traveling alone should ignore their instincts to be polite and err on the side of not letting an enormous man pull her through a van window and onto the human trafficking market.

OK, yes, this was becoming terribly awkward. She rolled down the window. "Can I help you?"

"Dr. Ramsay?" his voice boomed, practically shaking her van windows. "I saw you from the sweet shop window, thought I should come over and introduce myself proper."

Jillian sagged against her seat in relief. "Oh, thank you, but I'm just here to meet the mayor. Mayor Zed Berend?"

"Yeah, you right!" The man grinned again, showing perfectly white, razor-sharp canines. "You must be the League doctor. *Bienvenue*!"

Without an invitation, he yanked the van door open and pulled Jillian to her feet. He gripped her much smaller fingers in his very warm, very rough hand. Jillian stared up at him, mouth slightly agape. This was the mayor of Mystic Bayou? He looked more likely to be driving a long-haul truck route or forging lightning bolts on Mount Olympus. Who had dared challenge him for the position? Did he chew all of the ballots in half to remove his opponent from the election?

"Everybody's been waitin' for you to show up," he told her. "Well, they were waitin' for Dr. Montes, but they'll be just as happy with you. I can't say the whole town is gonna be thrilled that you're here, but like my *maman* always said, learnin' never hurt nobody. The guy at the League office said I have to sign a buncha papers before you can get started? Didn't I already sign enough? Y'all tryin' to steal my house and my firstborn?"

Jillian laughed at the rapid-fire questions. "No, but with Dr. Montes being replaced so quickly, the League just wanted to make sure the paperwork reflected the appropriate names, in case issues came up later."

Like the "issues" that came up with the cave troll study in the Reykjavik sewers. No one liked to talk about the incident that led to a League scientist being mailed back to headquarters in a shoebox, not even for training purposes. Jillian shuddered.

"What happened to Dr. Montes anyway?" Zed asked. "He was plenty keen to hit the ground runnin' and then he just stopped callin.'"

Jillian chewed her lip and tried to compose an appropriate answer. Currently Dr. Montes was in a League-funded ICU, ten stories below the surface of London, recovering from a unicorn impalement to the gut. Jillian couldn't imagine what he could have done to provoke that response from a unicorn. Hector Montes was a senior member of the paranormal anthropological staff. He wrote an actual book on approaching and interacting with sapient creatures. How had Dr. Montes underestimated the will (or the ticklishness) of a creature as old as a unicorn? Had he become too arrogant to consider his subject's feelings? Or had his clammy hands, combined with breath that smelled of old coffee and gingivitis, pushed the unicorn into a panic?

Zed was staring at her, waiting for an answer.

"Oh, um, he ran into some medical problems and couldn't travel," Jillian said, smiling through the awkward lie. "It happens sometimes. But I assure you, Dr. Montes trained me in field work. I'm fully qualified to handle this."

He jerked his shoulders. "Oh, I'm sure y'are, *cher*. No worries. You've probably taken dozens of these research trips, right?"

Jillian cleared her throat. "Well, not exactly."

Zed paused and tilted his enormous head toward her. "How many have you taken?"

Jillian pursed her lips and admitted, "One."

Zed asked, "One before Mystic Bayou?"

Jillian shook her head. "No, just this one."

Zed's cheerful demeanor faded. "You've never done this before?

"I was heading out on my first assignment in South America before the League called me back in and redirected me here," she told him. "I know what I'm doing. I've studied the process over and over. I've collected and interpreted other researchers' data... This is just the first time I've done it on my own."

Zed practically deflated, leaning against her van with a dumbfounded expression. "I don't mean to be rude, but I just don't know about this, Doc. It was hard enough to talk my neighbors into participatin' when they knew that they were gonna be dealing with an expert. I just don't know how people are gonna react to someone your age, without any real experience."

"Well, we don't exactly have to include that information when I introduce myself. I'm not planning on handing out copies of my CV to random citizens," she protested.

Zed's cheerful demeanor returned full force. "Good point, smart lady. If I've learned anything since takin' office, it's that less is more when it comes to information and your public image. It's why I deleted my Facebook. Nothin' good can come from your constituents knowin' you unfriended them."

The radiating heat of his hand on her elbow as he led her into the building had her sweating even more. She cast a mournful look over her shoulder, to the van, where fresh clothes and her trusty dry shampoo were waiting in her bag.

Zed shrugged. "We'll just have to see how things play out. I'magine you're pretty tired after all that flyin'. The sheriff says there's nothing like it, but I never took to it. Prefer to keep my paws on the ground, if ya know what I mean."

Zed flung the heavy wooden door open so fast Jillian didn't get a chance to study its carved details. He led her into an open office, divided into sections with lines on the floor. One corner was marked "Revenue" with gold lines. Another was marked "Public Works" with green lines. "Schools and Social Services" was marked in red and "Everything Else" was marked with blue.

"The whole parish government operates from this one room?" she marveled.

Zed seemed very pleased with himself as he pointed to the various departments. "Well, I get my own office over there and the sheriff gets his own office on the opposite side. But it works just fine. We don't have much room here and it keeps things simple if we can just holler at each other from across a room instead of callin' and leavin' messages and cursin' the voicemail and gettin' so stirred up you can't remember why you called in the first place. End-of-work was a little while ago, but usually this place is a beehive. Theresa Anastas keeps us all lined up and running without smacking into each other. She runs the Everything Else department. Gigi Grandent—she's a seventy-seven-year-old human and more terrifying than I could ever be—runs Public Works with an iron fist. Mr. Chiron retired as superintendent, but he's good at keepin' the schools running. And Betchel Boone may be a bit of *couillon* but no one can keep the books balanced like he can."

"Boone? As in the family that seems to own all of the businesses in town?" She gestured toward the street.

Zed grinned. "Caught that, did ya? Nice enough folks, the Boones, I suppose. They're used to gettin' their way and get plenty fired up if they don't. We let 'em throw their money around because it makes them happy and keeps the town in clover. And then we mostly get things done when they're not around."

A sharp voice interrupted him, "Not all of us are like that, Zed."

Zed's cheeks went a little pink under his beard, when another man, lean and tall with almost preternaturally sharp cheek bones appeared in the doorway marked, "Sheriff's Department. Check all firearms with the mayor before knocking." The man's light hair was shorn close, which only emphasized his large, amber-colored eyes and sharp features. He was wearing a tan police uniform and a gun belt that seemed to have a lot of "extras," but Jillian wasn't super-familiar with law enforcement gear... And she was staring at his narrow waist, which he had noticed. Awkward.

Zed shook off his embarrassment by flashing that winsome grin again.

"'Course not. Sheriff, you are the exception to all the rules," he said in a condescending, teasing tone. "Dr. Ramsay, this is Sheriff Boone. Sheriff, this is Dr. Jillian Ramsay."

"Sheriff, I'm pleased to meet you." Jillian did not reach out to shake his hand, another etiquette issue. Some species of the supernatural world, like the Irish spriggans, could lose their glamour when touched by humans, so casual physical touch with strangers was taboo. Also, some species, like the rainforest-dwelling *nagual* were extremely prone to colds and therefore a little germaphobic.

The Sheriff said nothing. He simply stared at her with those strange eyes of his, as if he was categorizing her every freckle and flaw.

Zed sighed. "I told you all about her, Boone. Twice. This is the doctor that's gonna be studyin' how well we run things in our little town, so she can help other little towns do the same," Zed said, in a tone that was probably meant to evoke some sort of friendly response.

Instead, the sheriff growled, "Seems to me that those towns should figure that out for themselves."

Jillian scoffed, "Well, that's an interesting approach to inter-species cooperation."

The sheriff crossed his rangy arms over his broad chest. "Never said I planned on any approach."

Zed cleared his throat. "Doc, you got those papers for me to sign? I'll leave you two to your howd'ya do's."

Jillian reached into her enormous canvas shoulder bag, handed him a carefully labeled manila envelope full of reprinted paperwork. Zed opened the sheaf of official documents and beamed at her. "I get to use my official mayor stamp. I love doin' that."

Boone muttered, "To a point that might embarrass any other man."

Ignoring the sheriff, Zed strode into his office. Jillian turned her head toward the sheriff. The hair elastic keeping her thick blond mop off of her neck gave up the fight. It snapped and her hair fell around her face like a slightly damp gold curtain. The sheriff's eyes flashed and not with annoyance at the mayor. There were actual rays of light shining behind his irises. Which she now realized were longer, and narrower than average, like a cat's. He had to be a shifter of some sort. The mayor also had "double corporeal forms" written all over him, for that matter. But there were far too many varieties to guess just from eye shape or build. From what Jillian understood of shifter etiquette—or any other sort of etiquette, really—it was rude to ask someone, "so what are you?"

So, she would just have to wait.

"Sheriff Boone. Do you have a first name? Is there a reason the mayor doesn't seem to use it?"

The sheriff cleared his throat. "'Course I do. I'm Bael Boone. And the mayor doesn't use it, because he likes to needle my ass at every opportunity."

"I sure do!" Zed called from the next room.

"I'm sorry. Did you say *Bill* Boone?" she asked.

"Bael."

Jillian repeated what she heard, "Bill."

"Bael."

Jillian shook her head. "I don't understand. It's *not* Bill?"

The sheriff was starting to look annoyed, or, at least, more annoyed. "No. Ba-el."

"I could swear that's what I'm saying."

"No, B-A-E-L. Bael."

Jillian would admit that, at this point, she was needling him just a little bit. She had an excellent ear for accents, but very little patience or politeness left in her.

"Sorry about that. I guess it will take me some time to adjust to the accents."

Bael sniffed, "Well, it will take us just as long to get used to yours."

Jillian watched the sheriff's angular face carefully. Clearly, he was amongst the people who were "not all that thrilled" with Jillian's presence in town. And given the Boone family's apparent stranglehold on the town's economy, that pricked at Jillian's distrust.

No, she was a scientist. She wouldn't let preconceived notions or her discomfort in having someone attempt to stare through her skew her opinions.

"Well, I'm here to stay, Sheriff, at least for a while, so you'll have plenty of opportunity." She smirked at him.

Bael jerked his shoulders. "I just don't see the point in it, is all."

Jillian's brows drew together. "Your town represents one of the few settlements where supernatural creatures from nearly all cultures live and work together in relative peace, and have for generations. The League expects humanity to stumble on 'the secret' of the otherworldly any day now. The Loch Ness monster can't hide from Google maps forever. And when one domino falls, so will another and then another, until everyone knows that it's all real. Werewolves, fairies, shifters, spirits, mermaids, witches, all of their fairy tale nightmares come true. Don't you think it would be better if they had information on how other communities overcame their differences instead of running around in a blind panic and well, act out the whole 'War of the Worlds' phenomenon all over again."

Despite her impassioned speech, Bael was not moved. "I'm just sayin' that no good has ever come from people havin' the answers handed to them."

Zed rushed back out of his office, the papers flapping sloppily as he moved. "All done 'cept for the last one, which has to be signed in front of a witness. Sheriff?"

Bael sighed, "Hold on."

The sheriff very carefully reviewed each page...to the point where Jillian became concerned about his reading comprehension.

Zed seemed endlessly amused by Bael's insolence. "Bael hates it when I boss him around. He's hated it ever since we were kids. But I just remind him that his job description includes "other duties as assigned" tacked right there at the end, with an asterisk, and then he has to do it. Because the asterisk says, '"assigned at the Mayor's discretion."'

Bael's eyes flashed angry gold again. "Mighty big words from the guy who needed flash cards to remember his swearin' in speech."

Zed's grin should not have been as proud as it was. "I put the 'swear' in 'swearin' in.'"

Jillian cleared her throat. "Sheriff, that's a pretty standard cooperation agreement between the League and the town of Mystic Bayou. Because of your unique population, you are a perfect case study for assimilation tactics. You guarantee me access to any archives or census information I need and attempt to smooth the way for me with the locals. I agree to be as unobtrusive as possible and show you all of my research before I leave town. Mayor Berend was pretty specific about that."

"Maybe where you're from, people give their name without a care, but I want to know what I'm signin'," Bael drawled, placidly flipping through the paperwork.

"He's got this whole thing about not givin' his *true name,*" Zed whispered dramatically. "The whole family's that way. Their first names are all nicknames. He refuses to tell me and I'm the closest thing he's got to a best friend!"

"No, you're not." Bael shook his head, blithely reading through the contract.

Zed grinned. "I've been guessin' for years though. I'm pretty sure his true name is somethin' like *Marion.* It's OK, buddy. Marion can be a boys' name, too."

Jillian looked to Bael, who silently shook his head.

It took several more minutes, but Bael finally signed the last page of the contract. A quick motion caught Jillian's eye, and she barely restrained a gasp as Zed sliced his palm open with a wicked sharp claw on his right hand. In a business-like manner, he pressed his mayoral seal onto his palm and then the paper, leaving a livid red crest next to the signature line.

Jillian shook her head. "Oh, that wasn't...necessary."

Zed frowned at her as he signed his name with a plain old Bic pen.

"Now, the local ladies' guild wanted to throw you a proper crawfish boil to welcome you to town," Zed told her.

Jillian gulped, audibly. "That's very generous of them."

Bael rolled his eyes a bit. "Don't get excited. People around here throw a party every time somebody loses a damn tooth."

Zed shot Bael a warning look, the first truly dark expression she'd seen on his face. The predator's threat sent a cold shiver down her spine. If Jillian had those icy eyes glaring at her that way, she might have added soiled pants to her list of hygiene issues. Bael simply jerked his shoulders.

In a pointedly pleasant tone, Zed said, "I thought that might be a little overwhelmin' for you straight out the gate. I figured you'd rather get settled in and get some sleep, get your legs under you, before you have to make your first impressions. We'll schedule your official welcome sometime this week."

"That was very thoughtful of you," she told him. "Thank you."

Zed grinned at her, putting his passive (no-longer-bleeding) hand on her shoulder. "You need anything, you just let me know."

Bael growled ever so slightly. Jillian frowned at him, and turned back to Zed. "Directions to my hotel would be appreciated."

Zed gave her shoulder a friendly squeeze. "Oh, we've got you set up with a real nice place."

"I didn't see a hotel on my way into town. I don't suppose there's a Holiday Inn one street over, that I just didn't see?" she asked.

Bael scoffed and Zed glared at him, then ratcheted up his smile a few degrees before saying, "Like I said, we've got a real nice rental place for you. It's got a lot of...charm."

Jillian found his pause before the word 'charm' to be highly suspicious. "Okay, I guess working out of a house will be more pleasant than working out of a hotel. Can you give me directions?"

Zed was half-way to a nod when he said, "Yes, but I can't help you get there right now. My *maman*'s expecting me at her place to fix her freezer. I keep tellin' her that she's overwhelming the twice-cursed thing, stuffin' two whole deer carcasses in there. But then she glares at me and reminds me winter's always around the corner and we need to think about puttin' on hibernation weight. And then, I shut up because there's nothin' scarier than a Berend woman when she thinks you're not listenin."

Jillian tilted her head and stared at him. "It's May."

Zed shrugged. "Winter's always just around the corner to *Maman*. But the Sheriff here can lead the way to your place. He's one of your nearest neighbors."

Jillian shook her head. "I don't want to be a bother. If you just give me directions, I'm sure I can find it."

Zed snorted. "Not likely. The roads 'round here twist and turn and only half them have the right signs, because the fair folk think it's funny to switch 'em around. I can only find my place because I've lived here my whole life. But the Sheriff will be happy to give ya the full police escort, won't ya?"

Bael only glared at Zed.

"Other duties as assigned, Bael," Zed reminded him.

Bael exhaled deeply and for a second, Jillian swore she could see smoke rings billowing out of his nostrils. "Follow my car."

2

JILLIAN

Mayor Berend had not been kidding about the twists and turns. The sheriff had only led her a mile out of town and they'd already gone over two bridges and passed four signs marking a "crick." She had no idea where she was.

Now they were farther away from town, she could see that there were a lot more houses than she expected. Not all of them were on stilts, but most of them backed up to the water. The bayou was clearly the center of life here. From the aerial maps she'd glanced at on her layover, she saw that the town's population centered around an area of the bayou called la Faille. Dr. Montes's notes stated that the citizens regarded la Faille as an almost sacred site. While there was a wealth of solid land in that area, no building or home was built within ten miles of it.

From what she could gather, she and the sheriff were heading northwest of la Faille...and out of town, for that matter. She was starting to wonder if he was leading her away so he could kill her and hide her body in the swamp, when he turned on a road called Possum Tail.

Who was in charge of naming things here?

There were no houses on Possum Tail, just endless trees bearded with Spanish moss. It would've been really pretty, if she wasn't worried about the whole murder thing.

The squad car slowed and turned onto a gravel drive that she would've passed by entirely if she was on her own. There was no mailbox or marker, just a pause in the greenery. Slowly, a pale house breached the trees like some ancient sea creature.

Unlike every structure they passed so far, this house was several stories stacked on top of each other like a wobbly, metallic wedding cake. At one point, the house had been painted blue, but weather and runoff from the metal roofing had turned it an uneven pewter gray against the backdrop of lush green.

A bay window, another feature she hadn't seen on any of the other houses, extended over the best view of the Bayou. A cupola served as the bridal "topper," and Jillian thought she spotted a telescope edging over that cupola's window. Each level had its own wrap-around porch, and someone had taken the time to hang baskets of geraniums from the eaves. And while they were very pretty, she was more grateful for the layer of privacy they would provide. A collection of mismatched rocking and lawn chairs were circled around a wooden platform that extended from the ground floor onto the water. Jillian slid out of her van, gaping up at the sight of her temporary home.

"What is this place?" she marveled, setting her sunglasses on top of her head.

Sheriff Boone was already out of his car, a set of house keys in his hand. "Folks around here have called it *la maison de fous,* the Fool's House, since I was a boy. My mama told me it was built by a sea captain named Worthen. He fell in love with a sea sprite who'd made her home in the Bayou. He built the house here so he could be close to her. But she never returned his love and he was so heartbroken and distracted that he built his house at all these crazy angles, not paying one bit of attention to how his neighbors' houses were built."

She opened her van's backdoor and slid a large duffel bag onto her shoulder. "Sounds like one mean mermaid."

Without her asking, the sheriff picked up two of her larger boxes of equipment and balanced them in his arms as if they weighed nothing. "Well, the captain had the last laugh. He married a local witch woman who loved him beyond reason, fed him queen's cake every day and gave him six children. And the house has stood more than hundred years. The town doesn't have the heart to let it fall down after all this time, so people around town pick up the little repairs whenever they can. We just replaced the stilts before Miss Lottie died."

Jillian glanced at the wooden supports that kept the house a good six feet above the waterline. Even though they looked pretty sturdy, the idea of sleeping over water wasn't exactly comfortable for her. "Miss Lottie?"

Bael nodded, the last of the sun's dying light gleaming off of his close-shorn golden hair. "The last of the captain's great-great-grandchildren. She was the closest thing we had to a doctor. She had her nurse training from a fancy *drole* school in the city, then her mother was a white witch, so she could heal our kind through either means."

Jillian stopped, adjusting the weight of the bag on her tired shoulder. "What's a *drole* school?"

Sighing as if he was very put upon, Bael took the bag and carried it, too. "It's just the way we refer to the outside world. *Drole* means funny or bizarre, and not in the nicest way, to be honest. It's a little bit of an insult. And to us, everything in the outside world is weird, so anything to do with the outside world is *drole*."

Jillian hummed. "So you're like the Amish, but with more fangs."

He nodded. "Yep."

"Really expected more of a response to that," she muttered as she slid the old brass key into the door.

Compared to the tent she'd expected to spend the next four months inhabiting, the house was luxurious. Sure, it was rough. The walls were whitewashed. The floorboards, also whitewashed, were worn smooth by years of foot traffic. Cooking and heating seemed to be handled with a large cast iron stove in the middle of the parlor, which was...intimidating. She would probably be spending a lot of time at the pie shop.

From what she could tell, there was no air-conditioning. The captain-architect had built screened grates into the higher floors, to vent the warmer air as it rose. But the wooden furniture was polished and well-cared for. Miss Lottie had left hanks of fragrant herbs hanging from the summer porch. And someone had recently cleaned the windows. She could see the vinegar soaked newspapers in the kitchen trash. The porch ceiling was painted a soft blue-green called "haint blue," meant to keep away both evil spirits and insects. Small animals carved from peach wood stood sentinel on the window sills. Several more hung from live oak trees surrounding the house. In some cultures, peach wood was used to ward off negative energy. Miss Lottie clearly wanted to keep her home free of bad vibes and had used a lot of cultural touchstones to do it. Even though she was still a bit skeptical about such things, that was a comfort to Jillian. She needed all the good vibes she could get.

Jillian had been dropped into a fairy tale cottage. She wasn't sure whether to take notes and photos or start removing the talismans before she broke one and cursed herself. She was vaguely aware that she had a big dopey grin on her face when she turned and saw the sheriff staring at her with that inscrutable golden gaze of his. She cleared her throat and tried to adopt a more professional expression. "Um, how much French do people speak around here? Will I have a hard time getting around, communicating? I'm pretty fluent in Spanish and a little Portuguese, which was appropriate considering I was on my way to South America. But French has always eluded me."

"Well, not nearly so much as in other towns. We're not a true Cajun community. When the first creatures moved here in the 1800s, there was a small Cajun settlement, just a few humans. Some of them inter-married with our kind, others stayed separate. We kept some of the French sayings, and most of us have accents, to varyin' degrees. We have some of the same food customs, but we've also mixed in our own traditions, our own flavors and our own languages from the places where we come from. It's a big mess sometimes, but it works for us."

Bael turned his gaze upwards. "Your bedroom is the first on the right on the second floor. The back door doesn't always catch, so make sure you lock it at night."

"So, this isn't one of those small towns where people pride themselves on not locking their doors?" Jillian asked.

Bael shoved his hands in his pockets. "Our crime rate's pretty low, but there's a good chance of varmints gettin' in if you leave the door open."

Jillian's expression was vaguely amused. "Varmints?"

He jerked his broad shoulders. "Nothin' wrecks your mornin' like findin' that a possum's tossed your kitchen. Speaking of which, Zed's mama stocked the fridge with basics for you."

Boone nodded toward a white-and-rust-colored icebox straight out of the 1950s. Frankly, she was surprised the floorboards would support that much weight. "That was very sweet of her."

"Well, mama bears never want to see starvin' cubs."

Jillian wiped at her forehead, sticky with the day's last layer of drying sweat. "I'm sorry, I've been traveling for almost twenty-four hours now and I'm having a hard time focusing. Is that a euphemism? Are there really going to be bears and possums outside my door?"

"Bears? No," he said, though she noted he paused just a little too long before eliminating the possibility. "Possums? Maybe. Gators? There's one out there right now."

"What?" she glanced out the back window to a pair of reptilian eyes through a layer of green algae on the water. "Oh, no, no, no. That thing can't get into the house, right? It can't break through the floor boards or anything?"

He snorted. "I think you've been watching too many scary movies. Gators don't want any more to do with you than you want with them. Just stay out of the water, unless you're with someone who knows what they're doing. And make sure you don't change in front of the windows," he told her, nodding toward the gator. "He could be a *magie*."

She rolled her dark blue eyes a bit. "Very funny, hazing the over-tired new girl in town who doesn't know any better."

"I'm not kiddin'. The Beasleys are gator shifters and they're known peeping Toms," Bael insisted.

Jillian recoiled from him. "Oh."

"But they live on the other side of town," he added. "So... yeah, you shouldn't change in front of the windows."

"Thank you, I'm sure that will help me sleep at night."

The corner of his lips twitched ever so slightly. And for a second, she thought he was going to make a remark about how she slept through the night, but he stayed silent, which was even more unnerving.

"Also, what does *magie* mean?" she asked.

"It means 'magic' in French. It doesn't quite cover the nature of all of the creatures in town, but our ancestors considered anything that wasn't human to be magical. It's a lot easier to spit out than supernatural. And it prevents a lot of confusion and offense, because no one is left out."

She nodded. "That's nice."

"Well, I'll leave you to it." Bael paused and handed her a pair of business cards. "Zed said he'd come in the morning and help you get into town. He thought it would be easier than you trying to drive yourself around for the first couple days. Don't try to drive in to town on your own. You *will* get lost."

"No problem. I'm stubborn, not stupid."

He muttered, "Well, that's a comfort."

She pulled her phone out of her bag and frowned at the lack of bars. "If I try to call you on my cell, will I get a signal?"

"Closer to town, maybe, but not from here. You're gonna need to use Lottie's, er, landline." He nodded toward a large wooden box hanging on the wall, complete with an ear trumpet and an honest-to-God hand crank.

"That's intense," she said, frowning.

"Miss Lottie was of the 'if it works, don't fix it,' frame of mind. The phone worked for her mama and her mama before her, so why change?" he said.

Jillian's mouth turned down at the corners. "Do I have to yell for the switchboard operator to connect my call?"

"I'll be honest," he said, shaking his head. "I don't know."

She walked out with him, to retrieve the last of her equipment from the van. Despite the last-minute change of plans, she'd carefully organized her equipment into boxes by rate of use, then attached a list to each box, listing its contents. It wasn't much beyond video and computer equipment, but she felt better knowing that she could easily find what she needed.

"I'll help ya." He reached for the heavy camera bag she was slinging over her shoulder.

"I've got it," she insisted. "I'm used to hauling it around by myself. Look, you seem to think I'm not prepared for this situation. I'm a professional anthropologist. I know enough not to cause trouble where I go, not to try to change anything, and not to offer insult when I can avoid it."

"The problem bein' that you don't necessarily know what's an insult here and what's not."

Her smile was sticky sweet as she asked, "Is it an insult to say 'thank you for leading me to my house, now please feel free to...'"

Her voice trailed off as she stepped forward, her eyes wide as saucers as the red, blue and green bottles hanging from Miss Lottie's trees lit up against the purpling twilight. Fireflies filtered out of the swamp grass, adding a touch of whimsical energy.

"Are those... That's not electrical!" she exclaimed, glancing back at him, grinning wildly. "Those are ghost lights."

Bael slid a Mystic Bayou Sheriff's Department baseball cap onto his head. "Let's just say that any spirits that tried to trespass around Miss Lottie's got put to good use. She said it was her way of being 'environmentally conscious.'"

"I've never seen anything like it," she breathed. "That's amazing."

Bael cleared his throat and opened his car door. "Yeah, well, so much for 'professional and prepared.'"

Her jaw dropped as he slid into his seat and turned the key in the ignition.

"Zed will be by in the morning." He rolled down his window as he backed down her gravel drive. "Get inside and lock your doors, Miss Ramsay."

"It's Doctor Ramsay!" she called after him. She sighed. "Eh, he didn't hear me."

Though she was an independent, capable woman fully in command of all of her faculties, Jillian rushed to the front door of the house and locked it behind her. Capable was one thing. Alligators were another.

She leaned her head against the solid wood of the door. Without competing noise pollution, the sounds of the bayou closed in around the house—the grinding hum of cicadas, the tap of mosquitoes throwing themselves at her windows, the throaty chorus of bullfrogs. It was an interesting contrast to the sirens and traffic noise she was used to in DC. Then again, she wasn't sure she could sleep in total silence. She hoped her brain would accept bugs and frogs as a substitute.

All she wanted was a shower and something resembling food and then a bed. She would sort through her equipment and clothes tomorrow. She double checked the back door to make sure it was locked, picked up her computer bag and suitcase and carried them up the rickety wooden stairs to the bedroom. She paused on the stairs and hung her head. She hadn't even asked if there was a shower. What if all she had was a metal washtub and a sponge?

A search of the second floor, and then the first floor again, confirmed that there was a "water closet" tacked on behind the kitchen, but no tub. She thought about going to the third floor, but the markings on the door told her that had been Miss Lottie's ritual space and it was better not to mess around up there unprepared.

"Dr. Montes, wherever you are, I hope your unicorn wound is very itchy," she grumbled, scrubbing a washcloth over her face and arms before stomping back into the bedroom.

Miss Lottie's old room was another challenge. While it was a very pretty room with a high ceiling and the big bay window, her bed was a swing. She wouldn't necessarily call it a sex swing. It was a simple wooden frame, hanging from silvery-white ropes suspended from the ceiling. The frame was covered in a feather tick mattress and a beautiful old log cabin quilt. It did however make Jillian wonder about what Miss Lottie got up to in her golden years.

She sighed, rolling carefully onto the mattress, yelping as it swayed back and forth. This was only slightly less ridiculous than a waterbed. Who even came up with this idea? This could not be good for a senior citizen's back.

She rubbed her eyes with her fingertips, waiting for her bed to still. How was she even going to begin this project? She'd given Bael Boone a reasonably good speech about her professionalism, but she'd planned a small study on a single species. This was a large-scale study of multiple species, cultures and how they interacted. And she had no idea where to start.

Every day brought the world closer to the discovery that humans were not alone on Earth. The International League for Interspecies Cooperation, a cooperative organization founded centuries before by a particularly open-minded group of shifters and humans under a far less corporate name, was hoping to hold on to secrecy for just a little bit longer. They were preparing for the worst. The administrators at the League wanted to use Mystic Bayou as a template for other communities on how to live cooperatively with multiple species and cultures. The League wanted to show humans that there was nothing to fear from the otherworldly. That shifters and fae and other creatures had lived among them for centuries and for the most part, humans had been unscathed. Her study would provide guidance for communities all over the world. It would be cited in academic journals and discussed in anthropology classes for decades to come. This was a huge opportunity for her. So why did she have such a bad feeling about it?

Why had the League chosen to send her? There were several other qualified anthropologists on staff. Yes, Dr. Montes had technically been her mentor, in that he'd led the review committee for her doctoral project, but he hadn't given her any practical training. The most interaction they'd had was when he read the first few chapters of her thesis on how the internet would eventually affect the how people saw ancient folklore, and he directed her to an online database called *faefolkwiki*. Why wouldn't they send someone with more field experience?

She took a long, deep breath and forced herself to focus on the positives—the professional opportunity, Zed's cooperative attitude, the comfortable house as opposed to the tent she was expecting. She would be fine. She knew the interview techniques. She knew how to archive. She knew how to organize her information. It was just like her old friend, Mel, said, when life sends storms your way, smile and whisper, "fuck off" in the storm's face, then go on your merry way.

Mel's advice was not like other people's advice. He said that his proverbs didn't translate well from the original ancient Japanese. Jillian suspected it was his liberal use of the F word.

She'd like to tell Bael Boone to jump directly into the nearest creek. Who did he think he was, devaluating her research before she'd even started? If Zed supported her efforts here in the bayou, who was Bael to tell her to get done and get gone? And the way he'd looked at her when she'd seen the spirit lights, that disdain and contempt for her enthusiasm, had sucked the joy out of witnessing her first bit of real magic. Sure, she'd read about witchcraft in theory, but this was the first time she'd seen a spell actually work. It was everything she'd hoped for, beautiful, useful, harmless. How dare he take that away from her?

The real fly in the proverbial ointment was that he was so damned attractive. While the mayor's hulking frame and craggy good looks certainly weren't repulsive, Bael's leaner build and diamond-sharp cheekbones were more her speed. If she was the gooey romantic type, she would probably fall in love with his voice alone. There was a soft purring timbre to it, like he was telling her secrets while on the edge of falling asleep. The man was seduction personified in polyester uniform pants.

And that was a difficult look to pull off.

But cautionary tales abounded during her internship with the League, tragic examples of researchers of either gender who got involved with their subjects. In fact, there was even a capstone seminar at her internship, entitled "Strategies to avoid getting intimately involved with your subjects." When fairytale creatures and humans got involved, it never seemed to work out well for the human. The human usually ended up cursed or pregnant with a baby that would try to eat them.

And then there was the Tate of it all. She couldn't ignore the Tate issue. He'd really done a number on her ability to date like a regular person.

Watching the ceiling sway over her head, she took a deep breath and counted to ten. She could do this. She could get through this study, make connections within Mystic Bayou, while living in a fairy tale witch's cottage, write a stunning report, and provide help to hundreds of communities. All while avoiding under-the-pants involvement with Bael Boone.

As she drifted off to sleep in her swinging bed, Jillian made a list of tasks for the next day. She would call Sonja and try to get more information about Dr. Montes's "medical problem." She would talk to the mayor and work up a list of important families to interview. And she would buy one of those noise machines that played traffic noises and sirens because the bugs were not getting the job done.

3

BAEL

Bael leaned back in his office chair, eyes sore from staring too long at his computer screen.

A series of smoke rings rose above his head, a sure sign of frustration in a Boone. He'd researched for weeks to prepare for Dr. Montes's arrival. He'd done a full profile of the anthropologist, becoming deeply acquainted with the man's professional and personal history. Dr. Montes had been arrogant and pompous, like a lot of academics, but he didn't seem to have any agenda beyond advancing his own career.

Bael had been comfortable with that. A greedy man could be trusted because he could be counted on to be greedy. Dr. Montes would do what was best for Dr. Montes. He would do nothing to risk his ability to stay in Mystic Bayou and continue his research, even if it meant surgically attaching his lips to Zed's ass cheeks. Bael knew how to direct that sort of energy.

This woman, Dr. Ramsay, pretty as she may be, was an unknown quantity, and that made her dangerous. While she had several articles published in all the right academic journals, her online presence told him very little about her private life. Her only social media footprint was a spartan Facebook page, but her personal information was limited to her hometown in Ohio and where she went to school. She didn't even list a workplace, because the general public wasn't aware that the League existed.

Her timeline seemed exclusively devoted to keeping up with old school friends, referencing their weddings and children and moving for new jobs. There was nothing about her own life, no pictures out with friends, no selfies from her favorite travel spots or posts waxing poetic about her favorite overpriced coffee. There were no mentions of her spending habits. Her relationship status was "Nope." He didn't know Facebook did that.

How was he supposed to predict the behavior of an unknown quantity? What sort of havoc could she wreak on the town? Bael had expected a middle-aged, balding greedy man with a strange predilection for posting on not-as-anonymous-as-he-believed fetish forums for pony play. Instead, he'd gotten a fair maiden with golden hair and a smart mouth.

Still, she'd been out of her element in Mystic Bayou's City Hall. That much had been clear. Between her fatigue, the rough environs, and Zed being, well, himself, she'd clearly been uncomfortable. But she hadn't been rude or cold, as some city folk were wont to do when they visited the bayou. And she hadn't let Bael push her around. He had to give her some grudging respect there. He'd tried not to be charmed when she explored Miss Lottie's house, but she had that look on her face, the look of someone seeing magic for the first time. That was pretty rare in a town where everybody was some sort of magical.

But again, that sincere curiosity could be dangerous without constant monitoring. He wouldn't interfere with her studies because Zed wanted her there and Bael respected the mayor's decisions when it came to the town's well-being. Bael just had to get her out of town before any of his people got hurt. That was his job, protecting those who lived in Mystic Bayou. And if that required some none too gentle nudging to help speed her on her way out of town, well, so be it.

"Are you cyber stalkin' our fair doctor?"

"What in the furry fuck?!" Bael shouted, turning to find Zed standing over him. He snarled at his old friend, who never failed to point out that he was technically his boss.

Zed grinned and made lazy swipes at the smoke rings, reducing them to nothing. For a big guy, Zed was way too quick and quiet on his feet. It chapped Bael's ass that he never heard Zed sneak up on him. That was another problem with living in a town where everybody was special. No matter how responsive your senses, someone else was quieter.

"What? No, I was just tryin' to get some sort of feel for her!" Bael exclaimed.

Zed's lips curved into a smirk beneath his thick dark beard. "I'll bet you were."

Bael tossed an empty coffee cup at Zed's stupid face, which, of course, he caught before it could do any damage. Bael scoffed. "*Couillon*. I'm just trying to understand who she is, so I can keep her from making too much trouble before we 'encourage' her out of town as quick as possible."

Zed scratched his beard, considering. "She doesn't seem like the troublemaking type to me. *Pauve ti bete* looked like she was about to faint off her feet yesterday, and she couldn't have been sweeter."

Bael chuckled. "Said the man who still talks to the ex-girlfriend who threw an air-conditioning unit through his bathroom window. While you were in the shower."

Zed jerked his massive shoulders. "Eh, Pam's OK. She just hated it when I talked during *Grey's Anatomy*."

"I'm just saying, look at your history. Your tolerance for crazy is pretty high. You're not the best judge."

"You may have a point," Zed conceded. The chair across from

Bael's desk protested with a mighty squeak as Zed's heavy frame flopped into it. "But considerin' you have *no* history, I don't think *you're* the best judge."

Bael rolled his eyes. It wasn't that Zed lacked a point. Bael had no romantic connections in or out of town. He'd barely dated beyond the expected schoolyard flirtations. When his parents died, leaving him their fortune at a relatively young age, he'd realized what a disaster it could mean for him and his kin if he chose the wrong woman as his mate. Bael wanted a woman who was a treasure, a rare jewel that he couldn't just find under any log in the bayou. And while many of the local women were perfectly lovely—other than crazy Pam Beaulieu—he hadn't found the woman to capture his interest. So Bael was, as he liked to put it, selective. Zed called him "frigid," but Zed could be a real asshole sometimes.

"So how much does she know?" Bael asked.

"Almost nothing. She's a completely blank slate, which could work out better than Dr. Montes anyway," Zed said, waggling his heavy, dark brows.

There were rare moments when Zed's cheerful sunny bullshit gave way to his more predatory nature. Bael was grateful this was one of those occasions. "Montes had pretty definite ideas how things were gonna run. Ramsay's unsure of herself, which we can use to our advantage. She seems pretty open to lettin' you 'guide' her through the introductions. Just introduce her to the more presentable families in town, then get her out of here."

"Why are you so worried about her bein' here, Boone? We're gettin' a more than fair payoff in exchange for participatin'. The kind of help we can only get from the League."

Bael gave him a hard look. "You know why I'm so worried. There are things happening here that we don't want the *magique* community *or* the human community to know about."

"And we've talked to the families affected. They know what to say and what not to say. No worries."

"You know people around here love nothin' more than good gossip. Do you really think they'll be able to resist?"

"I'll do damage control," Zed swore. "I'll distract her with town archives and local folklore and shit. You know I can be charming when I wanna be."

A molten spark of jealousy burned through his gut. He didn't want Zed charming Jillian. He wanted Jillian very far away from Zed and his...charms. The instinct to acquire, to hide the good doctor away from Zed and all other competing males, was as surprising as it was overwhelming. Bael felt the familiar warmth of his other form sliding over his skin. He had to close his eyes and think his calming thoughts to keep from shifting. His office wasn't big enough to contain his other form.

But to Zed, apparently, it looked like he was on the verge of losing his temper. "Just be nice to her, Bael. There's no use in bein' rude. It's not her fault she's here. She planned on bein' in South America right about now, talking to perverted dolphins or some such thing. I'd like to think we're an upgrade from that, but what do I know?"

"What?"

Zed shrugged. "Never mind. I'm gonna go retrieve Dr. Ramsay from Miss Lottie's, take her to breakfast, get her started meetin' people."

"Fine, fine," Bael muttered. "Go. I'll talk to the ladies about settin' up the boil for this weekend. There's bound to be some sort of fight over how many peppers to use, and what kind. There's always a fight over peppers."

Zed stood, jingling his keys. The flash of metal caught Bael's eye. "Wait, did you ride your bike into town today?"

"Yeah, why? Girls always dig the bike."

Bael pictured Jillian on the back of Zed's ridiculous overcompensation of a motorcycle, with her arms wrapped around his back and her legs wrapped around his... He shook his head. "Nope."

Zed scoffed. "What do you mean 'nope?'"

Bael stood, slapping his cap on his head and picked up his keys. "I bet that lady's never been on a bike in her life. And it's not safe to have some newbie on the back of your bike with the way you drive."

"What's wrong with the way I drive?"

Bael threw his head back and laughed, and then suddenly stopped, pointing at his face. "As the guy who writes the tickets in this town, I'm just gonna make my unimpressed face at you."

"Smartass," Zed scoffed.

"I'll go pick her up and drop her off here. You go get your truck. And you just, try to act like a normal person...for a few days."

Bael shook his head and walked out of his office.

"I'm not a normal person," Zed called at Bael's retreating back. "I'm awesome!"

BAEL ARRIVED at *la maison de fous* to find Jillian standing on the dock, taking pictures of the bayou with a camera that probably cost more than his squad car. Her hair caught the morning sunlight, gold shining with facets of copper and bronze. Precious colors, all. He moved closer, drawn by those glimmering strands, dancing in the light breeze. The wind delivered her scent to nostrils already flaring with interest—soft and clean, with floral undertones and a hint of ...old paper? How much time did this woman spend in libraries that the smell of books had seeped into her skin? And why was he enjoying it?

She turned toward the noise of his footsteps, a bright smile on her face until she saw who was there. The death of that smile, the way the joy just leached out of her face, pricked at his heart. He hated to be the beast taking that smile from her. But it was probably better this way. The fewer attachments she had, the quicker she would want to leave. The less she liked him, the less tempted he would be.

"I found my bathtub," she said, nodding to a beaten copper tub on the back porch, right next to a "sun shower," a tall wooden shower stall with a washtub mounted over it. Rainwater, which was always plentiful here, collected in the tub and was warmed by the sun. When the bather was ready, they slid a panel aside and the water drained over them through little holes in the washtub. "You could have mentioned that it was outside."

Bael took his sunglasses off and tucked them in his uniform collar. "Well, the house was built before indoor plumbing. You were lucky to get the water closet tacked on. And Miss Lottie was what you might call, 'a free spirit.'"

Jillian giggled. "A septuagenarian who slept in a swinging bed and showered outdoors? You don't say."

"Well, there are benefits to not having any neighbors for miles. If it makes you feel any better, there's a screen on top of the washtub that keeps leaves and critters out of it," he said, pointing to the top of the shower.

"Oh, yes, I do feel better now that I know I won't be sharing my shower with a raccoon," she said, scoffing. "I just have to be worried about perverted alligators. Wait, Zed said you were my nearest neighbor. How close are you?"

"Not close enough for you to worry about your showerin' habits," he deadpanned.

"Well, I'm sure I wouldn't have to worry about that anyway," she shot back. "I thought the mayor would be picking me up."

Bael cleared his throat. "He had something come up, so he

sent me ahead for you. He'll meet you at City Hall. Did you eat yet?"

She nodded. "I need to write Zed's mom some sort of a thank-you note for leaving all those groceries in the fridge. Also, for not leaving deer in the fridge."

"Aw, Clarissa wouldn't want any sort of special thank you," he insisted. "Just the next time you bake something, take any extra by her place. She's got a big sweet tooth."

"Bake something." She winced. "Right..."

"Not much of a homemaker?" Bael guessed.

Jillian bit her lip. "I can feed myself. I just wouldn't want to put anybody else at risk."

"That's very kind of you. Now, get your gear and get in the squad car."

"Do I get to ride in the front or back?" she asked dryly.

He slid his sunglasses back on his long nose. "Depends on how much lip you give me."

THE LADY DOCTOR was oddly quiet on the way in to town, taking notes in a little Moleskin notebook she kept in the ugliest canvas shoulder bag he'd ever seen. While she'd smelled quite pleasant yesterday, even after her extensive travel, today was different. He could smell the nerves rolling off of her as they rolled closer to town, a sharp metallic note under her natural flowers-and-old-books scent.

He thought maybe he liked her better when she was quiet. But he would never admit it aloud. Because she would probably hit him with that ugly-ass bag.

He parked in front of City Hall, and she seemed to be taking in the town for the first time all over again. She jotted down more notes in that precise, blocky handwriting of hers. He didn't take that many notes and he investigated actual crimes—not much in the way of major crimes, but that was beside the point.

She was still being quiet as she stood in front of the heavily carved front door of the hall, a scene depicting all of the creatures represented in the local culture, living cooperatively, with a dragon flying high, very high, above them. The same scene was reflected in the fountain behind them, common creatures scuttling about below the majestic dragon.

It probably wouldn't surprise the doctor to find out that his great-uncle Barnard had commissioned that door years before. Uncle Barnard had never been a subtle man.

The door opened and out stepped yet another Boone cousin, Balfour. An instinctual growl rippled out from Bael's belly, which only made Balfour smile. Balfour had the Boone look about him. He was lean and tall with thick dark hair and tawny eyes, but there was a tilt to his full mouth that made him look like he was perpetually smirking. And ever since they were kids, Bael had been plagued by the urge to knock that smirk off his face.

And when Balfour saw the human woman stepping aside to let Balfour by, his smile ratcheted up a notch. Bael had the overwhelming impulse to throw a jacket over Jillian's head before Balfour saw the way her hair glinted in the sun.

"Well, hello there," Balfour purred, reaching for her hand.

"Hello." Jillian took a step back, which only increased Bael's estimation of her intelligence and self-preservation skills.

"Bael, introduce me to your charming companion." Persistent Balfour with his long Boone limbs kept reaching for Jillian's hand, even as she moved away. Ignoring this, he plucked it from her side and bending over to kiss it.

In his most deadpan tone, Bael said, "Balfour, this is Jillian Ramsay, PhD, she's an anthropologist working for the International League for Interspecies Cooperation. Jillian

Ramsay, my cousin, Balfour, who has no qualifications or accomplishments to recommend him."

"Aw, Bael, young Miss Ramsay won't know you're just kiddin," Balfour cajoled in a much thicker Southern accent than Bael used. Bael noted that Balfour called Jillian, "Miss Ramsay" and not "Dr. Ramsay," which would definitely stick in Jillian's craw. Now it was Bael's turn to smirk.

Balfour leaned in ever so slightly, and though Jillian would never recognize the gesture, Bael saw the subtle inhalation. Balfour was taking in her scent. Like horses, once a dragon had a person's scent in their nostrils, they would always hold that scent. It came in handy when one was trying to track down humans who stole from their hoards. Balfour would keep that little piece of the blond doctor with him forever. And that made Bael want to break his cousin's face. "Oh, yes, my mama told me you would be conducting interviews all over town. Be sure to put me on your schedule. I would love to give you an intimate look into the life of the Boone clan."

Jillian smiled politely, but Bael noticed that she ever so subtly swiped her hand against her jeans to wipe off Balfour's kiss. Also, she was leaning away from Balfour, nearly resting her head on Bael's chest in her attempt to make space between them. When Bael didn't step away from the accidental intimacy, he could practically see the wheels turning in Balfour's head.

Bael's slightly younger cousin had been a thorn in his side for decades, always jockeying for position in the family, always trying to curry favor with their grandfather, Baldric, while making Bael look bad. It had started with feigned injuries at family gatherings, claiming that Bael had been too aggressive during their hatchling games. And now he was whispering to the uncles and Baldric that Bael's unnatural fixation on his non-entrepreneurial profession made him unfit to inherit any of the family's hoard. Balfour liked to cluck his tongue and sigh about "poor Bael," whose parents died before they could finish raising him.

So it was with no small amount of pride that he watched Jillian brush Balfour off as if his oily charm slid right off of her.

Jillian cleared her throat. "Thank you, I'll be sure to seek you out when I need information from you. If you'll excuse me, I have an appointment with the mayor."

Balfour opened the door for her with a flourish. "It was enchanting to meet you."

Jillian jerked the corners of her mouth in an awkward little smile and scurried into the office as quickly as she could. Balfour let the door close behind Jillian and nodded at Bael's uniform. "Cousin, still indulging in your little eccentricity, I see."

"Yes, public service is such an odd impulse," Bael retorted.

Balfour sneered. "It is for a Boone. At least Betchel is in there tracking the family's wealth, making sure it's going to the right places and getting paid back. You're just wasting all of your time, running after people, keeping them from hurting themselves. I just don't see the benefit in it."

"Which is why 'service' is the operative word," Bael told him.

"Yes, well, to each their own, I suppose," Balfour drawled. "You coming to the family meeting?"

Bael nodded sharply. "Yes, Friday, at the moon's rise. I'll be there."

"Grandfather seems very close to making his decision. I would hate for you to miss it when he passes all of that gold into my hands." Balfour smiled nastily.

For his part, Bael tried to look impassive. "If that's his decision, I'll respect it. And if that's not his decision, I can't think of one person who will be surprised."

"And will you be bringing your intriguing new companion?" Balfour asked.

"You leave her out of this, Balfour, I mean it."

Balfour tossed his hair, ever so casually. "I don't blame you for lowering yourself, to take up with a human. She's simply incandescent, even wearing those frumpy clothes. When you're not looking, I might try to steal her for my own hoard."

"She'd destroy you in a week," Bael snorted. And he was only half-bluffing. Balfour had never been known for his patience and, eventually, Jillian's multitude of questions would make his head explode. She would be the only damsel in history to rescue herself through persistent interviewing.

Balfour's eyes flashed, a sickly amber instead of Bael's own gold. "Well, it would be amusing to watch her try."

Smoke rose from Bael's nostrils, and he could feel the fire climbing up his throat as he growled, "Stay away from her."

Balfour smirked, raising his hands. "Touchy touchy. You know the code. *Lose not one coin.* The same applies to your little friend. If you don't want to lose her, don't give me the opportunity to take her."

Balfour slid on his sunglasses and walked toward his shiny red pick-up truck, whistling some obnoxious tuneless song.

"Prick," Bael grumbled, flame bursting forth from his mouth like a belch and singeing the carved wood sprite dancing across the door. Sighing, he patted out the smoking sprite and yanked open the door.

Boone walked into the office to find Zed had greeted Jillian with all of the overwrought enthusiasm of a labradoodle. He dragged her around the room, introducing her to Aiden Rhys, a *fenodyree* who ran Public Works, and his own cousin, Betchel, who worked in Revenue. Jillian held him at a distance, shaking his hand politely again, seeming overwhelmed by the attention. Some small part of Bael enjoyed her civil rejection of Zed, who was well-known for his skills with the female variety. Bael wondered what sort of attention Jillian got from men where she was from, and whether she held them off so courteously there.

Zed looked over his shoulder, frowned and waved his hand in front of his face, which was their private signal for smoke rings rising above Bael's head. Bael startled and waved the smoke rings away. Betchel smirked at him. Bael silently bared his teeth, because apparently, all of his cousins were trying to piss him off today.

Zed ushered her through the door of his office, a temple unto all the things that Zed loved—Zed, his mama, Zed, hunting, Zed, fishing with his bare hands. Mostly Zed.

Picture frames and trophies covered every spare inch of space not occupied by his massive desk, which he had carved himself out of a fallen oak. He tried to call himself Zed Oakendesk, after watching the *Hobbit* one too many times, but Bael refused because a man shouldn't come up with his own nickname.

Zed shoved Jillian into one of his very comfortable office chairs and then flopped into his own. "How exactly are you planning to conduct your study?"

Jillian seemed to roll her shoulders and put on her pleasant professional face. "I thought at first, I would approach it a bit like a census taker. I'll collect questionnaires. I'll make general observations. I'll document group social interactions and local traditions. And I'll gather anecdotal evidence. And I thought I would make appointments to interview families from all points in the paranormal spectrum."

"Is that how a typical anthropologist would handle a cultural study?" Bael asked. Both Jillian and Zed turned toward where Bael was standing in the door. Irritation flared in Bael's belly. Apparently, they'd forgotten he was there.

Jillian turned ever so slightly toward him, which eased the indignant burn in his gut. "Well, the interesting thing about paranormal anthropology is that we've had to create our own methods. Your cultures are like no other cultures on earth, so accommodations have to be made."

"And you know I'll be accompanying you on the first couple of visits, right?" Zed asked.

"Yes, just out of curiosity, are you offering that because you went to be helpful and smooth my way, or because you want to monitor what I'm doing?" she asked, sliding on a sensible pair of reading glasses that made Bael's mouth go dry.

Zed snickered. "A little of both."

"Well, you're honest. I'll give you that."

"Do you want to get started right now?" he asked.

Jillian nodded and pulled out a mini recorder from her horrible bag. "Sure, do you mind if I ask you a couple questions on the record?"

Zed's grin was a white slice against the dark of his beard. "I'd expect nothing less."

He glanced up at Bael. "You want to shut the door? I'd hate to get background noise from the office on her recording. Having the phone ringing in the background would be a real distraction."

Bael frowned. "Uh, sure."

Bael couldn't help but think that he saw Zed smirking a bit as he shut the door, closing Jillian in Zed's office. Bael was pretty sure he was going to find a way to punch Zed in the gut later, just on principle.

4

JILLIAN

Jillian's second full day in Mystic Bayou was no less exhausting than the first.

After a very thorough, hours-long interview, Jillian was so numbed by the amount of information Zed had given her on the town's history, politics, economics and traditions, all she could do was ask for a ride back to her rental house and press a cold beer bottle to her temple.

The beer was another gift from Zed's beloved *maman.* Seriously, if Jillian ever met Mrs. Berend, she might kiss her on the mouth. According to Zed, the whole family was pretty free with their affections, so she'd probably be okay with it.

Jillian laid out on the porch swing, watching Miss Lottie's spirit lights come to life one by one, and used a dictation app to try to organize her thoughts on what she'd learned that day. She kept telling herself that she would be inside before the sunset, but it was just so pleasant out here, with the heat fading out of the day and the smell of honeysuckle blending with the citronella candles she'd lit. The candles, combined with the haint blue paint and the geraniums, seemed to be keeping the bugs at bay.

According to Zed, and the messy sheaf of disorganized newspaper clippings and notes he'd handed her, the first supernatural settlers filtered into a place the locals called *le Lieu Mystique* early in the 1800s, just after New Orleans started taking off. Shifters, witches, sea creatures, and *magique* of all types were drawn to the little Cajun settlement because of a convergence of energy in the waters just beyond the outlying homesteads.

There was no explanation for the mystical vortex, no ley lines, no electromagnetic anomalies, no historical melees. The rift in the fabric of what kept their world separate from the dimension beyond simply was. And it attracted *magie* creatures like wasps to an open Coke can.

At first, the *magique* tried to pass as human, but there were only so many lies they could tell and stories they could make up when strange creatures were seen running through the swamp in the moonlight. It stretched the locals' tolerance of weirdness to the limit, and considering some of the Cajun traditions, that was saying something.

Eventually, a Berend, the shifter amongst them who was most likely to be able to defend himself from any attacks from the human settlers, met with the town fathers and revealed himself as a man who could shift into an enormous brown bear.

Jillian stopped her voice app and pulled out the mini-recorder, checking her notes for the time stamp when Zed told the town's origin story. She'd particularly enjoyed that bit. She found the right spot and Zed's gruff, warm voice poured out of the recorder.

"So my great-great-great-great-great-great-great-granddaddy dropped his drawers, changed his skin, and there he is, a big ol' bear, standing right in front of them, trying to shake their hands with his paw. Because my great-great-great-great-great-great-great-granddaddy was a bit of a smartass. One of the town fathers soiled his breeches while the others screamed about hoodoo and witchcraft and all another manner of nonsense. Finally, the one elder who still had some sense in his head, handed around glasses of homemade brew and told everybody to shut their faces. Then my great-great-great-great-great-great-great-granddaddy turned back into human and they all had some beers."

Jillian's voice sounded on the recording. "You don't always have to say it like that, you know. You can just say 'granddaddy.' I'll know who you mean."

"Yeah, I do," Zed had insisted. "More fun that way."

Listening to the recording, Jillian distinctly remembered the grin on Zed's face when he'd said this. Zed might have been a bear shifter, but he was also an enormous troll.

"Anyway, he assured the humans that their new neighbors had no intention of hurting them. That they only wanted to live quietly in a place where they felt comfortable and happy. And if the humans were willing to live in peace with them and keep their secrets, then the *magique* would share all of their knowledge and magic. The town fathers probably didn't feel like they had much of choice, given the number of fangs and claws on our side, but they agreed. There were some people who kicked up a fuss, of course, and those people either moved out of town or got too aggressive with the wrong *magie* and were never heard from again."

"There's always going to be that one guy," Jillian had observed.

"Yep. My great-great-great-great-great-great-great-grandaddy became the unofficial leader of the *magique*, and eventually the Berends took over leadership of the town. We're lucky that the people trust us to do what's right for them, I think we've done a fair job of it so far. Over the years, the humans calmed their asses down, especially when they saw how fae folk helped the crops grow, or how the healers kept their children well, and the weather witches kept the hurricanes away. And soon enough, their daughters started marrying our sons and our sons married their daughters. The line between their culture and *magie* culture faded and it just became 'our culture.' It's like a big gumbo, everybody gets to know each other in the pot. We have Mardi Gras and Samhain and blood moon howls. And the Friday fish fries, can't forget those. Technically, my family's German and I've had more andouille in my lifetime than I've ever had schnitzel. Everybody gets along, more or less, but we're a town just like any other little town. We have our squabbles, but I think that's just people, no matter how human or inhuman you are."

"And where do the Boones come into this?" she'd asked. "Were they the only *magie* family that had any money? Or do they just really like putting their names on businesses?"

"The Boones didn't come to town until later. About a hundred years after my great-great-great-great-great-great-great-granddaddy-"

"Zed," Jillian sighed.

Zed had cackled loudly on the recording, and she could hear him open up a jar of honey-flavored lollipops he kept on his desk. He'd handed her one as a peace offering and took another for himself. "After we got everything settled down, the Boones, whose real family name was Bogen."

"Bogen?"

"Yeah, isn't that the scariest monster-sounding name you've ever heard?" Zed had exclaimed. "Anyway, they changed it to Boone when they passed through Ellis Island, and rolled into town in a fancy wagon. And the wagons kept coming for weeks, covered up like they were carting around Sigurd's left nut. They were the most secretive people that ever came to town. For one thing, my great-great-great-great-great-great-great-great-grandaddy-"

On the recording, Jillian sighed.

Zed continued as if he hadn't heard her, "Thought it was

strange that they changed their name so easily when they came to the States, as proud as they were. It made everybody wonder what they had to hide. Then they all lived separately instead of grouping together, like most families did. They threw up storefronts all over town, but none of them helped each other build or start up their new businesses. They were cold and competitive people, and they didn't make a lot of friends. And they seemed okay with that. But they did have a gift for making money, and the few times over the years the town needed it, the Boones were right there."

"And does their talent for making money play into their *magie* nature, or is that just a happy coincidence?"

Zed had squinted at her, grinning. "You haven't figured out his shifter form, have you?"

Jillian had pursed her lips in response.

"Really? Why don't you just ask him?"

"Because it's rude!" she'd cried. "And Bael already has some sort of grudge against me! And you'll notice I didn't ask you what he is *directly*. I just hinted for clues."

"And you don't want to admit that you can't figure it out."

"The man gives no outward signs," she sighed. "You're clearly a bear shifter."

"What do you mean, *clearly*?" Zed exclaimed, obviously insulted.

"You mentioned hibernation three times this morning. And your name is Berend."

Zed grumbled, "Still feels like profiling."

Jillian's tone was far too intentionally guileless when she asked, "So what are the Boones?"

Zed had grinned at her while he countered, "I thought it was rude to ask."

Jillian huffed. "It *is* rude to ask. But I thought you might tell me out of respect for the tentative friendship we've built between us."

Zed crossed his massive arms over his equally large chest. "No, you not knowing is more fun. I think I like this game. It makes the little vein on your forehead stand out."

Jillian had growled. "Fine. Enjoy my discomfort. So if the Boones have all of the money, why don't they run things around here?"

"Oh, they had no interest in running the town. They don't devote their time to taking care of people, but they enjoy watching money make other money. They definitely enjoy having the town beholden to 'em."

"But you and Bael seem to be pretty close friends," Jillian had said.

"Oh, sure, I love the big dumbass, but you'll soon see for yourself he's not exactly cut from the same cloth as his family. He's the only one that seems to care about other people and the fact that they exist. So, years ago, my family got together with the Boones and agreed to split leadership of the town. The Boones made sure the town could keep the lights on, so speak. The Berends took care everything else."

"Interesting," Jillian noted.

"Yes, my great-great-great-great-great-great-great-granddaddy would have been proud."

"Is there another more mature city official I can talk to?" Jillian had asked.

"Yeah, but they're not nearly as entertainin' as I am."

On the porch swing, Jillian shook her head. She knew she was supposed to stay impartial, but she was quickly becoming fond of Zed. Yes, he was attractive in a rough-hewn way that was intimidating as hell. But he was also a kind man, one who seemed to see her as some sort of cute younger sister he was supposed to tease and torment.

Jillian checked the time on her phone and noted in a rare moment of cell phone-to-tower serendipity, she had more than one bar. She quickly dialed Sonja's number and prayed the connection lasted.

Sonja Fong was an office administrator, performing daily organizational miracles for the higher ups at the League office. Jillian knew they were destined for close friendship from the first day Jillian started with the League. Sonja had crossed the League's plush hardwood-paneled lobby to warmly welcome Jillian to her internship and then informed Jillian very quietly that she'd spilled part of her morning latte on her blouse. Jillian, embarrassed by her first-day gaffe, whipped a stain wipe out of her shoulder bag and dabbed the spot away. Sonja's dark eyebrows rose and she tugged open Jillian's shoulder bag, revealing a carefully organized – and labeled – array of pens, notebooks, lip balms, hand sanitizers and wipes, each in their own compartment. She closed the bag and said, "I'm going to like you, Jillian Ramsay."

They'd become roommates shortly after that. Jillian needed someone to take up the other half of her lease. Sonja needed to live with someone who wasn't certifiably crazy, as opposed to her last roommate who had set her closet on fire because Sonja forgot to take the cup out of the Keurig machine one morning. Which seemed like an overreaction.

While Jillian worked hard to maintain the façade of a poised professional, Sonja was effortlessly attractive, elegant and always in control—even when dealing with a crazy roommate. Jillian frequently envied the way Sonja, the daughter of a Chinese diplomat and a Russian physicist, managed to navigate her way through the politically treacherous waters of the League office. Attending some of the most vicious upper crust boarding schools available in the States, she knew enough not to involve herself in the interoffice blood feuds or get caught up in promotion squabbles. She did her job. She got her stuff done. She learned everything about everybody. And she looked freaking fabulous doing it.

After the day that she'd had, Jillian was grateful this wasn't a video call, because she didn't need to be faced with Sonja's unruffled perfection.

"Sweetie," Sonja sighed as she picked up the phone. "Are you okay? What time did you finally make it there? Did you get any sleep? Are you staying in a decent hotel? Do they have a Starbucks there? Do I need to have the National Guard airlift peanut butter cups and vodka to you?"

"No, no it's definitely rural but it's not...terrible," Jillian said, her voice rising an octave on the final syllable.

"You hesitated."

Jillian chuckled. "I'm aware."

"Seriously, are you okay?"

"I'm fine. I promise. The conditions here are not ideal, but it could be a lot worse," Jillian said, trying to avoid the octave waffling this time.

"Where are you staying?"

Jillian could hear Sonja moving around their kitchen at home, making herself dinner, and smiled. Sonja never did one thing at a time. She considered it an indulgent waste of precious hours. Jillian once caught her plucking her eyebrows in the reflection of their toaster, while cleaning out the crumb tray.

"A charming and comfortable little rental house," Jillian told her.

"On the edge of a swamp," Sonja added.

"It is swamp-adjacent, yes," Jillian admitted. "But still, I'm more comfortable than I would be in a tent in the jungle, so that's something."

"Are you upset that you're missing out on the study in Chile? I know you really prepped for it."

"Eh, the sex-crazed dolphins will still be there in a year," Jillian sighed. "This study takes priority. It will help more people. Though I am pretty curious about how the hell I got here in the first place."

Sonja took a long time to respond. "You're going to be pissed."

Jillian sat up on the swing. "All I know is that Dr. Montes got injured while interviewing a unicorn. Why would I get pissed about that?"

"Yes, Dr. Montes was injured while interviewing Thistlewaite, the oldest known unicorn in the world. In fact, he took a lot of trouble to arrange a special trip to Wales and hire a unicorn translator, who was willing to travel to a glen in the middle of nowhere," Sonja said over the clatter of a whisk in a saucepan. "Which we all thought was weird because he was supposed to be getting ready for this massive study in Louisiana, right? In fact, it seems particularly out of character for a guy who holds all the other anthropologists to such strict professional standards about logistical and mental preparation. I mean, he literally wrote a book on it. But he kept saying it would all be worth it once he got his hands on Thistlewaite. We all thought he meant in in a figurative sense."

Very slowly, Jillian said, "Sonja, honey, talk to me like I'm a layman who never spent time around supernatural creatures and has suffered a significant head injury."

If wincing had a sound, Jillian was pretty sure it would sound like the uncomfortable humming on Sonja's end of the line. "Dr. Montes's is apparently into something called 'pony play.'"

Jillian asked in a hopeful tone, "As in playing with My Little Pony?"

"As in he enjoys caring for and training a person dressed as a pony, during special naked happy fun time."

Jillian nodded, but could not produce an audible response.

Sonja asked, "You OK, hon?"

Jillian squeezed her eyes shut. "I'm trying so hard not to judge. And to figure out how this could possibly connect to Dr. Montes's injury, and yet I don't want to picture it."

"Well, according to what I could puzzle together from snooping through his email—"

"Yeah, you've received several interoffice memos stating you're not supposed to do that," Jillian noted.

"Well, people around here need to make their passwords more complicated if they don't want me reading their emails. I mean, honestly, the digits for their birth date and their dog's breed? Amateur hour," Sonja scoffed. "Anyway, Dr. Montes's emails made it pretty clear that his pony partner had recently opened the barn door and headed into someone else's corral."

"I beg you to stop with the horse metaphors."

Sonja continued as if Jillian hadn't spoken. "Dr. Montes got dumped by his pony partner, leaving him in deep personal turmoil. And apparently, the temptation of being near a real live unicorn with his beautiful iridescent white coat and ivory horn spiraled with gold, so soon after losing his equine paramour was just too much of a temptation."

Jillian pinched a bridge of her nose. "And he expressed this by tickling the unicorn?"

Sonja hummed. "Well, it wasn't so much tickling as...heavy petting."

"I'm showering outdoors in a swamp because my boss tried to fondle a unicorn?" Jillian exclaimed, nearly flipping herself off of the porch swing. In the distance, several birds took flight from the trees around the house, squawking indignantly. She could only hope that these were actual birds and not her shape-shifting neighbors who had just heard her yell sexually explicit nonsense.

Jillian was only snapped out of the white noise in her head by the sight of a nutria, an enormous rat-like creature, shuffling through her yard toward the water. It looked a lot like the Marsh Dogs mascot on the town welcome sign. The local mascot was a giant belligerent swamp rat. Of course.

"Why are you showering outdoors?"

"Sonja, please focus!" Jillian cried.

"Yes, you're stuck in the swamp because your boss tried to fondle a unicorn. Thistlewaite took exception to Dr. Montes's unwanted advances and used the only weapon at his disposal, his horn."

Jillian made a sound between laughing and crying.

"Got him right in the gut," Sonja added.

Jillian cover her face with her free hand. "I should have been a high school history teacher like my mother wanted me to."

"Sweetie, you don't like children."

"So my boss is a misguided groper who can't be trusted around anything equine, that is news I didn't expect. But why did the League send me rather than someone else?" Jillian asked.

"That I don't know," Sonja said. "Several people in the department put their names up to be considered, but without even interviewing anybody, they named you. Nobody in the office is talking about it. The board met in a closed session after hours, to discuss your appointment and that was it. There are no memos, and you know the board documents everything in memos. It's some big mysterious deal."

"Well, it has to be mysterious if *you* haven't figured it out yet."

"That's what I'm saying," Sonja told her. "Just do your usual stellar work and come back to civilization, so we can reap the rewards of your inevitable and enormous success."

"I'll do my best. I really miss you. The people here are nice but they're not you," Jillian said.

Sonja's teasing smile was practically audible. "So they're nice, are they? Anyone being particularly nice? Anyone of the male persuasion?"

"Decidedly not."

"That sounds like a story."

Jillian could practically hear Sonja's eyebrows waggling over the line. "No really, I've barely met anybody in town. The two people I've spent the most time with are this giant goofball of a mayor, who looks like he would gladly separate your spine from the rest of you if you touched his motorcycle, but is basically a man-shaped marshmallow. And the somewhat attractive sheriff, who seems to want to load me onto a catapult so he can launch me out of town at the earliest opportunity."

"Neither sounds like a bad option, if you're looking for a little temporary distraction," Sonja purred. "And you can use a distraction, sweetie. It's been years since Tate. You need to get back up in the saddle."

"Let's just stay away from equestrian metaphors for a while, OK?" Jillian retorted. "And Tate or no Tate, I'm not going to screw up my first field assignment by sleeping with the people who could literally run me out of town on a rail."

Jillian could almost hear Sonja's pout over the phone. "You're no fun."

"I'm not ready, Sonja. I can enjoy the view, but I'm just not ready for anything besides looking."

"Alright, sweetie, alright. Just promise me one thing."

"What's that?" Jillian asked.

"When you find the right man, one you are ready for, you will climb him like a tree."

Sure that she would never meet such a person, Jillian responded without hesitation, "I will. Love you."

"Love you, too. Call when you can."

Jillian hung up the phone, gathered her things and moved inside. It was well and truly dark now, and she didn't want to be caught outside with unknown creatures, natural and supernatural. While speaking to Sonja had been a balm to her weary soul, even mentioning Tate threatened to drag her into a gloomy mood. She put her papers on the kitchen table and opened the fridge inspecting the offerings left behind by the good Mrs. Berend. She made herself a plate of cold fried chicken and settled in to finish her notes.

Her stomach twisted at the thought of food, but she forced herself to eat. Tate Ashford—seriously, she should've known that they were going to have problems from the uptight name alone—had been her first serious boyfriend after college. Hell, he'd been her first serious boyfriend, period. She'd met him at a conference for oral historians. He hadn't been attending the conference. He just happened to be staying at the hotel at the same time as the conference, attending the wedding of a fraternity buddy. They met in the hotel bar, and for once, Jillian was "socially lubricated" enough to carry on a casual, flirty conversation with a stranger. He'd been charming and sweet, and seemed so interested in her background and her family. It turned out that he was from the D.C. area, too, and they'd arranged to go out to dinner when they returned home.

She'd been a dumbass of epic proportions. She thought the fact that he had the patience to agree to a date weeks later instead of pressuring her into a one-night-stand was a sign of character, that it made him boyfriend material. He certainly had the right resume for a significant other. He was a lawyer working for his family's firm. He came from old money in Alexandria. He didn't drink or smoke or spend excessive amounts of time watching sports.

So, it was easy for her to ignore the early red flags. He wasn't very intellectually curious and scoffed when she mentioned something that she'd read. He didn't take a lot of pride in his work. Every time she asked him a question about his role at his office, it became pretty clear early on that he was the living embodiment of her dad's old chestnut, that "half of the lawyers and doctors in the world graduated in the bottom half the class." That was always her father's excuse for not going to get an annual physical, but it also shed some light on Tate's way of getting by in the world.

He was perfectly happy to have her on his arm at firm functions or family parties, but he didn't seem that interested in her as a person. She was well-educated arm candy. He wasn't interested in what she did for living, until he sensed her hesitation in telling him anything beyond the fact that she worked as an anthropologist for a private historical foundation—the public cover story the League insisted on for all employees. He didn't care to know until she had the audacity to say "no" to him, and then he wouldn't let it go, asking her dozens of needling questions and becoming frustrated and resentful for her lack of answers. He couldn't stand her drawing a line with him.

He flip-flopped on a lot of things after that. He was fine with them staying casual, until she went on a date with a coworker and suddenly he complained that he felt betrayed by her interest in other men. When she expressed disinterest in moving in together, he demanded they go look at apartments, only to change his mind when they made appointments with a rental agent. Just when she thought she'd figured out where he stood on an issue, he'd change his mind and she was lost again. All the while he accused her of using him for his connections, of not appreciating him, of being selfish and not taking their relationship seriously. She was so busy trying to keep up with his moods, to fight through the constant cycle of gaslighting, that she didn't question whether he was wrong.

Soon, Tate's discontent grew to how she dressed, how she wore her hair, the stories she told at parties. She rationalized a lot, told herself that dating a man like Tate would naturally be more complicated than the college boys she dated. She thought that adult relationships took more compromise. But by the time Tate was done nothing about her felt safe or sure anymore. She'd always considered herself a confident person, someone who made decisions easily. Every time she so much as tried to choose a dress, all she could hear was Tate's voice in her head, asking if she really thought *that* was the way she wanted to look when they went out.

The final strike against the relationship was that Tate didn't like her friendship with Sonja. He repeatedly pointed out the differences in the two friends' appearances and told her that girls like Sonja didn't have friends like Jillian. He insisted that Sonja was only using her for rent money and all the favors she did for Sonja. He refused to see that Sonja took care of Jillian just as much as Jillian took care of Sonja. Sonja's response was to use her connections at the State Department to have Tate added to no-fly lists in almost every country and put him right at the top of the federal sex offender registry. She insisted that this was justified and appropriate use of force.

True to form, when Jillian ended things, Tate told her he was tired of her anyway and she'd never find anyone else who would put up with her. And then he showed up to her apartment door with an engagement ring, which he threw at her closed door when she refused it. He still periodically texted her to ask her out for "drinks or something" because he missed her, and then left angry voicemails an hour later when she didn't respond.

Work was the only thing Jillian felt confident in after the break up, so in the past two years, she'd thrown herself into it fully. This was great for her career and moved her up in the ranks of the League's anthropology department faster than any new employee had ever risen, but it also left her drab and gray and drained. It took Sonja and lots of time to bring her back to the Jillian that Sonja knew and loved. Sonja had given up dates with highly eligible men to stay home and watch movies with Jillian. She personally oversaw an overhaul of Jillian's wardrobe and pulled several strings to get Jillian an appointment with the First Lady's colorist. She slowly brought the nonprofessional side of Jillian back to life.

While Jillian was in a much better place now, she wasn't ready to date. She'd tried going out with some very nice—truly nice, not "surface nice"—gentleman the last few months, but it never extended beyond drinks or a dinner or two. She had odd little flashes of panic any time her date changed his mind about something. She walked out of a dinner once because her date expressed an interest in the salmon, but ended up ordering chicken. She just didn't trust her instincts anymore. Sadly, the better a man seemed on paper, the more she pulled away, because now she knew better than to trust anyone who seemed to be "appropriate boyfriend material." She feared any man she found profoundly attractive would turn out to be an emotionally abusive asshat.

Jillian was sure her dating luck would be the same here. She might have thoughts about any number of available, attractive men in the Bayou, and have some weird, inevitably confusing dreams about Zed, but that's where it would end.

"Right," she said, nodding decisively. "Problem solved."

5

BAEL

Bael ripped the completed speeding ticket from his pad and handed it to the tourist from Texas. The man had the bad luck to try to take a shortcut back from New Orleans to Dallas and wrong-turned his way right into Mystic Bayou. Even more unfortunate for the tourist, this was the second ticket Bael had written for him, and Bael was getting pretty sick of his shit.

Paul Shields had gotten lost and turned around so many times trying to find his way back to the interstate that he got frustrated and drove through the town's school zone at forty-five miles an hour. And he didn't realize he was in a school zone, because kudzu had grown over the sign for the Mystic Bayou Combined School. And he argued viciously about whether he should be held accountable for speeding because he didn't realize that he was near a school. And in a third unfortunate event for Mr. Shields, he was parked next to another sign that read "Slow Down 35 MPH Zone," so Bael considered that a moot point. Mr. Shields did not agree, so vehemently that he ripped up the ticket and tossed the bits in Bael's face, shouting, "I'm never coming back to your pathetic little suck-town again! My tax dollars pay your salary, you know!"

Bael fucking hated tourists. They so rarely made it into Mystic Bayou that Bael forgot how annoying and arrogant they could be. But he couldn't rip this jerk's head off and shove it up his ass, because that would raise questions. And he couldn't take him to jail on charges of destroying what was technically a court summons and general dickheadedness, because that would keep him in town. And in Bael's experience, speeding belligerent dickheads making a departure from Mystic Bayou kept its citizens and secrets safe.

"Mr. Shields, do us both a favor and take the ticket," Bael said, all carefully faked patience. "Neither one of us wants me to have to fill it out again. Just take the ticket and stay on County Line Road and you'll be out of our 'pathetic little suck-town' in no time."

"This is *bullshit*," Mr. Shields seethed, snatching the ticket out of Bael's hand. "You'll be hearing from my lawyer!"

"I look forward to it. I'll be sure to tell him that his client destroyed an issued citation after driving like a speed demon through a space occupied by school children and calling a sworn officer of the law a 'puffed up, small-town inbred bitch cop.'"

"You can't prove I said that!" Mr. Shields cried.

Bael gestured to his squad car. "Dash cams, sir. Even in pathetic little suck towns, we can afford them."

Mr. Shields punched the gas and sped away.

"Stay on County Line Road!" Bael called after him, smiling and waving. While his face was frozen in that fake smile, he muttered, "*Embrasse moi tchew*."

Bael needed peach pie, immediately. He knew that his aunt Bathtilda had a batch baking this morning and it was necessary for him to complete his shift without murdering someone. Unfortunately, it was only nine a.m., and Bathtilda insisted that pie was not breakfast. At least, not a complete breakfast. So she served it with bacon, which was why she was Bael's favorite aunt.

This wouldn't happen if Bathtilda would let him keep emergency pies in his freezer. But she insisted that her pies only be served in optimal conditions, and "no pie at all was better than freezer pie."

A familiar white panel van rolled by—at a safe speed—but Bael wasn't any happier to see it.

"God dang it," he sighed. "I just want my freaking pie."

He slid behind the wheel and flipped his blue lights.

The van window rolled down and Jillian looked decidedly annoyed about being pulled over. She was wearing a lavender button-up shirt that brought out the purple undertones in her eyes. Her hair was arranged in a loose bun on top of her head in concession to the heat. "I wasn't speeding, Sheriff. I was going five under the limit, even with the school zone."

Bael tamped down the tiny flare of pride he felt in her managing to spot the sign when other outsiders couldn't. Stern and professional, that was him.

"Dr. Ramsay, what are you doing?"

"Not speeding?" she guessed.

"What are you doing, driving around by yourself?" he demanded. "Zed and I asked you not to do that, remember? Because you'll get lost. And I'll have to spend my whole week looking for your body. And honestly, the paperwork involved would just be a pain in the ass."

She glared at him. "Well, Mayor Berend was supposed to escort me to my interview this morning, but he didn't come pick me up, he didn't call and explain why, and now I'm due at Earl Webster's house in twenty minutes. And from what I've been told, Earl's a real stickler about promptness."

"You should have called me," he insisted.

"You've made it pretty clear you don't support my assignment here."

Bael pinched the bridge of his nose. "Just follow me and don't miss the left turn onto the gravel road. It's tricky."

Without his super-hearing, he wouldn't have heard her mutter, "Very helpful."

While it wasn't exactly how he planned on spending his morning, he was glad that he happened upon her before she tried to make it out to Earl's. Thunderbirds preferred solitude, and Earl Webster lived in one the most remote corners of town. His home was nestled in a rare tree-covered rise above sea level, hidden in so much swampland that even Bael got turned around driving out there. He was surprised at the flush of panic in his chest at the idea of Jillian driving out there alone, and not just in the annoyed "making the effort to find her submerged van" way. The urge to call Zed and demand to know what the hell he thought he was doing not keeping his appointment with Jillian was very strong. But then Zed might start to suspect that Bael was doing so out of more than professional courtesy, and the mockery would be both comprehensive and merciless.

Bael spent the next thirty minutes constantly checking his rearview to make sure that Jillian hadn't taken a wrong turn. He parked the squad car in front of Earl's two-story house, built to get Earl as close to the sky as possible. Earl was waiting out front, because he couldn't stand to have people approaching his perch without him watching.

Jillian was introducing herself before she got the door fully open. "Mr. Webster, thank you so much for meeting with me."

She glanced at her van's dashboard clock. "We were supposed to meet ten minutes ago. That's ten minutes I won't get back in my day."

Jillian blushed all the way down to her collarbone and began to stammer an apology to the tall, broad-shouldered old man with skin the color of cedar. Bael interrupted her, yelling across the yard, "Aw, come on, Earl, what's that mean in the grand scheme of things? You got about ten minutes less to watch Price is Right? Give the girl a break. Not her fault you live out in the middle of the ass end of nowhere."

Earl stared at Bael. Bael stared right back.

Earl grumbled, "Fine. Come on in."

Jillian practically slumped against the van in relief as Earl turned and walked into his house. Hauling her ugly-ass canvas bag out of the passenger seat, she mouthed, "Thank you."

Bael realized his earlier panic feeling had been replaced by something much warmer and sweeter. And he would never, ever tell Zed about it.

BAEL KNEW why Zed picked Earl for her first interview. Earl was prickly, there was no doubt about that and he wouldn't just lay down and let Jillian walk all over him while serving her sweet tea. But Earl also had a soft squishy marshmallow center, underneath all that gruff. So once Jillian finally settled in, she would get some good information.

The whole interview process was fascinating to watch. It seemed a lot like plain old visiting, but by a paranoid person who was taking the time to record a casual conversation between neighbors. She asked Earl all of the little "getting to know you" questions—how long his family had lived in Mystic Bayou, where they lived before, who built the house they were sitting in. All questions designed to help Earl relax, and prevent defensive responses right from the start. Jillian's body language and voice were completely different, when she was speaking to Earl. She was relaxed and interested but not overenthusiastic or off-putting. It was like a dance. She flitted from one conversational topic to the other, connecting them and weaving them together so that Earl seemed to forget he was being interviewed and just relaxed into talking about his favorite topics. Bael hadn't seen such masterful verbal maneuvering since the passing of his own grandmother, the undisputed queen of Mystic Bayou's limited social scene.

Ten minutes in, Jillian had Earl serving her willow bark tea and showing her the wood carvings his family had been creating for generations, commemorating great acts of bravery. The Websters were sinfully proud of the carved wooden figures, but for Earl to show them to an outsider just demonstrated Jillian's heretofore unknown people skills. Also, there was the possibility that because Earl didn't actively provoke her like Bael, she felt compelled to be charming toward him.

"So, you clearly have quite a few grandchildren that you're not proud of at all," Jillian noted, nodding toward the dozen or so teenagers smiling out from framed photos on his mantel.

Earl chuckled. "Good fledglings, all of them. Beautiful and brave. A bit too brave, if you ask me."

Jillian cocked her head. "How do you mean?"

"They want to leave the bayou," he said. "Websters have lived here in Mystic Bayou for generations, since before the dragons moved in. They want to go to big cities, where they can see more and meet more people. But you can't make weather in big cities, not without someone spying on you. Too much light keeps you from really seeing the sky. And don't get me started on the damn cell phone towers."

"Is that a problem a lot of families are seeing? Younger people who want to move away from the Bayou?"

"Oh, I wouldn't call it a new problem. As a group, we get a family with a wild streak every generation or so," Earl said, jerking those enormous shoulders. "Last time around, it was the Beasley boys. They wanted to move to one of them gator farms in Florida and put on a show, pretending to be specially trained gators. The problem being that none of them were smart enough to make the move happen. My grandkids burn a bit brighter."

"So, the Beasleys just stuck around and pursued their careers in the voyeuristic arts," she muttered, jotting down some notes in her little Moleskine notebook.

Earl shot Bael a look, eyebrows raised, but then nodded. "You were right to warn her."

"And how does that make you feel? Your grandkids wanting to move away?"

Earl frowned at her, as if he was disappointed. "That's sort of a stupid question."

"I'm aware, but I have to ask it anyway," she said, not seeming offended in the least.

"Yes, it hurts. But I understand the need to stretch their wings and see new skies. I can only hope that when they've seen what they want to see, they'll come home."

"Is that your wife?" Jillian asked, nodding toward a photo in which a much younger Earl had his arm wrapped around a pretty blond woman with a broad smile.

"That's my Kat. She passed away a few summers back. She was a phoenix, a real firebird. You could see her for miles when she lit up. My girls take after me, but the boys take after her."

"Really?" Jillian's eyes sparked with what could only be termed "scientific ecstasy." "So, they're either thunderbird or phoenix? There's no crossover? I've read some theoretical papers on the subject, but the superna—er, *magie* community has been reluctant to discuss how hybrid genetics work."

Bael sat forward a bit on Earl's lumpy couch, watching her closely. Of all the human emotions, he understood the nuances of greed best. But when he looked at Jillian, he didn't see the hunger of acquisition in the brilliant curve of her smile or the tension in her hands as she gripped her pen. She wasn't calculating the price she could get for taking *magie* secrets back to the outside world. He saw the thirst of curiosity in her. She burned to know for no other reason than wanting to understand. The knot of apprehension that had gripped Bael's chest since the League proposed this project, slipped loose just the tiniest bit.

Earl rubbed the back of his neck with his long fingers. "Well, I don't know too much about genetics or papers. I just know when two different creatures mate, it takes a while to see where their young will land, usually by age twelve or so. Some kids are lucky and they get a mix of their parents' gifts. Some kids, like mine, show a strong affinity for one set of talents over th'other. Some get none. Everybody feels a little sorry for those kids, but we try not to treat 'em any different."

"What did your families think of you and your Kat getting together?" Jillian asked.

"Aw, at least we were in the same sort of family of *magique*. We were both sky creatures. Not as weird as the time one of Bael's cousins tried to elope with that chupacabra girl a few years back."

Bael shuddered. "We don't talk about cousin Barry."

"So, no one has a problem when the families intermarry? As long as they're not completely incompatible and/or goat-sucking monsters?"

Earl nodded toward Bael. "Oh, most folks don't have any problem with it. Some families are a little stricter, like the Boones. A little more worried about keeping the lines free of human blood. Others are happy to get some fresh genes in the pool."

Small grave lines bracketed Jillian's mouth for a moment, but then disappeared.

"So, going back to the subject of your grandchildren, what do you think you can do to persuade them to stay in the Bayou?"

"It's not my job to make them want to stay," Earl said, snorting a little. "Or their parents' job to make them want to stay.

If we to try to keep them here, it's only gonna make them fight even harder to leave and they'll resent us so much they won't want to come back. If they need to go out and see the world, I can't stop them. I can only hope they fly back when they see it's not all they hoped."

"That's very philosophical of you," Jillian said.

"Well, if that doesn't work, there's always bribery," Earl said, making Bael snort and spit his iced tea back into his glass.

It was almost an hour before Jillian seemed to feel like she had asked enough questions. She even answered a few about herself while Earl signed the necessary releases for his voice recordings. Jillian was from Loveland, Ohio. Her utterly human parents were living, but she had nothing to say about them beyond pleasantries about her mother hosting charity events while her father ran an industrial equipment company, whatever that was. She had no siblings. She'd left no husband or beau behind when she'd come to Mystic Bayou. And she very gently, but firmly, informed Earl that she was not interested in going on a blind date with his oldest grandson, even if it would keep him in the bayou. Bael wondered if she'd made up a false life, empty of attachments, as some sort of cover for her work in the League, or if she was the loneliest person he'd ever met.

Bael watched her as he helped her load her equipment into her van, trying to detect some hint of sadness about her. But the lack of family didn't seem to weigh on her. Was she one of those solitary creatures, like the harpies that lurked at the edges of the swamp, eager to be near the rift, but more eager to avoid contact with others? She didn't seem like an antisocial creature. She had good manners, tolerated Zed well enough, engaged Earl in lively conversation. Did she simply not need people?

"So did I pass?" she asked as they loaded their last bag into the van.

"Beg pardon?"

Jillian leveled a bemused, yet annoyed, look at him. "The test you wanted me to pass before you'd be willing to unleash me on the general population. That's why Zed only scheduled one appointment today, right? You joined me on my interview with Earl because you wanted to watch me. You wanted to make sure I wasn't going to take advantage of Earl, ask him leading questions, poke my nose where it didn't belong. So, tell me, how did I do?"

He stared at her, eyes narrowed. He really thought he'd hidden his agenda a little better. It was unnerving to have a human read him so easily. "Just fine. I didn't really pay much attention. I just stuck around so you wouldn't get lost on the way home."

Jillian dropped her sunglasses over her eyes as she jerked her driver side door open. Bael was struck by the urge to pull them off of her face, to get rid of any obstacle blocking his ability to see into her eyes. His hands twitched at his sides, but he gripped his gun-belt to keep them still.

She smirked at him. "Lead the way, then."

6

JILLIAN

Three days after she arrived in Mystic Bayou, Jillian finally met the matriarchs of local society. It was Saturday afternoon. Jillian was sitting on her porch, still wearing cotton sleep shorts and tank top because it was the coolest clothing she owned, drinking a Coke while she pored over information on phoenixes and thunderbirds. She'd done some previous research on thunderbirds in college, but had less experiences with phoenixes, *Harry Potter* references aside.

Their ability to shift was often connected with the cycle of life, destruction and rebirth, which sounded beautiful and terrifying all at once, shifting into giant many-colored birds that burned with blue fire. Sometimes phoenixes needed to burn and regenerate to heal themselves from injury or distress. Sometimes they burned to predict great calamities. And sometimes they chose to burn, just for the joy of it. Jillian wondered if the associations with flight and fate were what had made Earl's thunderbird side such a compatible match with his wife.

And Bael, where did he fit into all of this? It was very frustrating that she couldn't figure out his shifter form. She'd figured out that Dickon Macey was a garden gnome within five minutes of spotting him at the Food'N'Fuel. (There was a disappointing lack of red pointy hats, but an abundance of back and shoulder hair that resembled moss.) Why couldn't she figure out Bael's tells? How did he manage to tamp down all instinctual responses around her? How could he appear to be so utterly human, when he was clearly something more? And why was she too stubborn to inquire around? She couldn't walk out into town and throw a rock without hitting a Boone. She was going to have to ask Zed some sneakier questions to get better clues.

She sighed, pinching her lips together. Because her intelligence was more than a point of pride for her. It was her defining personality trait. And admitting that she couldn't puzzle something out was more of a blow than she was willing to admit.

She flopped back in the swing. Sonja was right. Jillian was going to have to either have her friend airlift her some batteries or the world's biggest Sodoku book. Otherwise, she was going to go crazy.

In the distance, she heard what sounded like thunder, and by the time she saw Zed's bike, it was too late to run inside for some more appropriate clothes. So, she was going to brazen her way through it with a smile.

She stood up, sliding her papers into their file folders so they didn't blow away with the breeze. Zed somehow managed to park his bike in the driveway while waving his enormous hand at her.

"Well, hey there, *cher*!" he called after shutting off the bike. He slid his aviators into his collar and waggled his dark brows. "You didn't have to get all dressed up on my account."

Jillian noted that he didn't wear a helmet. His only concession to safety was to tie his hair back out of his face. He slung his jean-clad leg over the bike and stood, stretching his back. He unclipped some bungee cords holding a file box onto his bike, then he crossed her lawn, hefting the box over his shoulder. His faded black t-shirt rose over some impressive abs, dusted with dark hair.

If she wasn't absolutely sure that it would turn out to be an emotional disaster of Pompeii proportions, she would take Sonja's advice and climb that man like a tree. For science.

He draped his heavy frame across her porch swing, thunking his heavy motorcycle boots against the railing. He put the heavy box in her lap. "Hey, there, *cher*. I brought you those census records you asked for. I mean, we haven't participated in a federally funded census in more than a century. But we do the League's version—household, number of people, any magie, that sort of thing. Just for the sake of keeping up with trends."

"Anyone ever tell you that the polite thing to do is call before you show up to a single lady's house?" she asked.

"I've found that most of the single ladies I know don't mind," he said, cocking his head to survey her bare legs.

"Well, this one does."

"You keep on being cranky with me and I won't take you to your party," he told her. "And it's all the way out at my *maman's* place, so we're gonna have to hurry right quick."

She winced. "A party?"

"There will be pie."

She frowned at him. "Do you think you can lure me to a stranger's house with baked goods?"

"It's really good pie," he told her. "And it will be a chance for you to meet a lot of people at a time, something I know you've been itching to do."

She grumbled, "Let me put on pants."

"The five little words no man wants to hear," Zed said, pouting a little.

JILLIAN HAD EXPECTED a few families to be gathered at Clarissa Berend's house for a simple cookout. Instead, it looked like the entire population of Mystic Bayou had parked their pick-up trucks on the overgrown lawn. The house was more of a stone mound with windows, a sturdy tin roof and a large steel door. It wasn't exactly welcoming, but it certainly looked like the sort of place Zed would spend his time.

Zed parked his bike along the winding gravel drive and it took a few moments for Jillian to release her fingernails from his back. The man drove like a demon, laughing into the wind and trying to carry on a conversation with Jillian as if she wasn't screaming herself hoarse into his shoulder blades. Zed didn't seem to mind. In fact, he seemed pretty amused by the fact that her legs didn't seem to be getting the message from her brain to unclench from around his waist.

"Your mother's house is made of stone?" she said, trying to make casual conversation as he stood up from the bike, taking her with him. "That's not typical of southern Louisiana."

"My daddy tried to offer her a house made of wood, and she refused him." He unwound her legs from his middle and lowered her to her feet. Smiling fondly at her, he unbuckled her helmet and hung it from the back of the bike. "Told him she wouldn't sleep in a crate. She would have a proper den or nothing. Took my daddy two more years, but he built it with his own hands."

"Well, a girl has to have her standards," Jillian said, wobbling slightly on her legs. "So how am I going to tell who's who tonight?"

"What do you mean?"

"Shifters look just like any other humans in most cases. Faes can do amazing glamours," she said, sounding slightly frantic. "How am I going to tell human from a *magie* in such a large crowd?"

Zed frowned at her. "Why is that important?"

"Because I don't want to offend people! This could be a cross-cultural minefield. If I try to reach out and shake the wrong hand, I could start some sort of inter-species incident, which will not only undermine the League's authority but hurt a lot of feelings."

He patted her already mussed hair with his huge hand. "*Catin.*"

"You better not have just said something bad about me in French. I have Google translate." She nudged an elbow into his ribs.

"Don't look it up on Google translate. I don't want you finding me later and hitting me with those bony little fists. In France, it would be an insult. Here, it just means I think you're a doll baby." Zed threw an arm around her shoulders and her knees almost buckled under the force of it. "We *magique* can sense each other. There's a sort of 'hair standing on end' awareness when you're in the presence of another shifter or a fae. It doesn't help you much, though. Just relax. We're so used to bein' all mixed up that we don't hold you to a strict etiquette. Just treat everybody politely and you'll be fine. Not the icy politeness you use on Bael, but the sweet, funny girl you are around everybody else."

"Thank you for noticing."

She could hear the rumble of conversation from the backyard, even as Zed led her around the formless perimeter of the house. A dozen huge picnic tables had been arranged in two columns in grass that had been recently mowed. Lanterns and geraniums hung from cords strung between the cypress trees, giving the yard a festive, fragrant air. And while the yard was crowded, Jillian realized that a good portion of the buzzing she heard wasn't conversation. It was pouring out of neatly kept beehives Clarissa had arranged along the perimeter of her property.

The scientist in her tried to catalogue the various species crowded into the yard, but it was difficult. Sure, there were hulking shoulders here and the flash of a tail there, but so many of them were so carefully buttoned into their mundane forms that she couldn't tell human from shifter. They were old. They were young. They were every shape and color. The diversity warmed her heart, but confused her eye.

Suddenly, she was rushed by several middle-aged women wearing aprons over their jeans and camp shirts. Her cheeks were pinched and her hair was patted and she accepted it all with grace because she *would* make a good impression, dammit. Also, there were a hundred or so people in the backyard and they all seemed to be staring at her.

Clarissa Berend stood out from her slighter neighbors, a broad-shouldered woman with an ample chest. If the smoky eyes and wild dark hair streaked with silver hadn't given away her connection to Zed, the fact that Clarissa hugged Jillian so hard that she heard a rib crack certainly did. Stepping out of the hug, Clarissa took Jillian's hands and spread her arms away from her body so she could do a full head-to-toe inspection. "Oh, aren't you just a little doll? So pretty, with that gold hair and those nice birthing hips."

Jillian arched a brow. "I'm sorry?"

"Don't be offended," Zed muttered out of the corner of his mouth. "*Maman* considers that to be a high compliment."

Clarissa smiled at her, just as winsomely as her son. "Are you married? Are you engaged? Do you have a serious boyfriend?"

Zed did not seem at all distressed about his mother's line of questioning. "*Maman*'s determined to marry me off. I'm lucky there's no such thing as a shifter dating site. She'd sign me up without my knowledge or consent."

"I have some people looking into it," Clarissa said dryly.

"But I thought bear shifters were matrilineal. Don't you want Zed to marry a bear shifter female, so he can be part of a line?" Jillian asked.

"And she's smart, too!" Clarissa crowed. "Look at her! Yes, *bebelle,* we do trace our families by the female line. And yes, years ago, I hoped that my son would do the right thing and find some nice bear girl to marry. Now, all I want is for him to settle down with one girl—*any* girl—and make me some grandbabies before I'm too old to enjoy them."

"Well, thank you for your consideration, Miss Clarissa." Jillian had noticed that no matter how old a woman was or her marital status, all women in the Bayou were called, "Miss First Name." It was a mark of respect, an acknowledgment that you were close enough not to use last names, but not on even enough ground to be on a first-name basis.

"I really think you two would suit each other," Clarissa said, squinting as if she could see the future. She placed Jillian's hand in Zed's and stepped back. "Yes, I can see it now. You two would make me some beautiful grandbabies."

Zed quirked an eyebrow at her. "We could give it a try."

Jillian let go of his hand and smacked his chest.

"She hit me, *maman,*" Zed gasped. "Is that really the type of woman you want me marryin'?"

Clarissa lifted her dark brows. "If she's gonna keep you on the straight and the narrow? Yes."

"Well, while I don't think I'm ready to be your daughter-in-law, I'm pretty sure I like you," Jillian told her. "And I've been meaning to thank you for stocking my fridge before I got to town. You're a life saver. I don't know what I would've done in those first few days without that fried chicken of yours."

"Well, right back at you, you sweet thing," Clarissa cried, slipping her arm through Jillian's and drawing her toward a trestle table where two other women were laying down full newspapers.

Zed and Clarissa had Jillian clasped between them as Zed hollered. "Y'all, crowd round now, and meet Miss Jillian. She's the lady from the League I told ya'bout. She's a real sweet gal and smart as a whip. If she asks you any questions, answer whatever you want and show your manners about what you don't. She interviewed Earl just yesterday and he's no worse for wear."

"Didn't hurt one bit," Earl called, winking at Jillian, who waved back.

Zed put his arm around Jillian and squeezed her to his side with just as much strength as his mother. "I'm sure she's real eager to meet everybody, just let her get a plate before you rush her. Now, everybody, bow your heads and say your 'thank you's' to whichever gods you serve. And then pull up a chair and pour out the pots because I'm starving!"

Jillian watched as each citizen bowed their heads and observed a moment of silence, answering some of her questions about how people from so many religious backgrounds were able to co-exist. She'd noticed a distinct lack of churches in town, which was an oddity in a region where churches were a cornerstone of the community. She wondered how long it had taken for the citizenry to reach a relatively easy peace over private observations. She pulled out her Moleskine notebook and made a note to ask Zed later.

She looked up to find both Zed and Clarissa looking down at her with exasperated fondness. "My boy was right, you don't ever turn off that big brain of yours, do you?"

Jillian pressed her lips into a thin, somewhat apologetic line. "No, ma'am."

Snickering, Zed led her to a newspaper-lined table in the middle and handed her a beer, refusing to hear arguments that it wasn't professional for her to drink at a community event. Bael and Earl lifted a metal mesh pot out of an iron cauldron and onto the table—without protective gloves, she noted. They tipped the steaming contents of the pot onto the table and the whole yard smelled of lemon and spice and seafood. She spotted crab, shrimp, crawfish and potatoes and corn and her mouth began to water. She hadn't eaten since a hastily made grilled cheese around lunch time.

Jillian slid onto one of the picnic benches and followed Clarissa's example of tucking a large dishcloth over her collar.

"So how are you settling in out at Miss Lottie's?" Theresa Anastas asked, her soft Mediterranean accent standing out starkly from that of her neighbors. Theresa was a tall, stately woman with a thick head of dark chestnut hair shot with silver. She kept it wound around her head in a complicated braided crown. "I hope you're comfortable. She was very house-proud."

"Oh, it's very peaceful out there. I've never slept so..."

Theresa suggested, "Suspended?"

"Yes." Jillian nodded. "I've never seen a bed hung from a ceiling before."

Theresa preened just a little. "I helped Miss Lottie install the bed. She had some insomnia and thought the rocking would help her fall asleep. That's my silk in the ropes."

"Your silk... You're an arachnaed!" Jillian exclaimed. "How interesting to meet one this far west! I read that you don't leave Greece."

"We don't very often, but my own dear mother couldn't resist the pull of the rift. And having so many hands does help me run the department of Everything Else, plus occasionally serving as dispatcher for the sheriff." Theresa flashed a smile that featured way too many teeth and the air around her shimmered with the energy of shifting. Suddenly, she had eight shiny black, articulated arms spreading out from her sides like wings.

Jillian gasped, delighted, and clapped her hand over her mouth. "That's amazing! Would you be willing to sit down and talk to me about your experiences here in the Bayou?"

"Of course. I was a little hurt that you hadn't asked yet," Theresa said, nudging her with one of her many elbows and sliding a spiced red potato toward her with her fourth arm.

People filled up the table where Jillian was seated, introducing themselves, their families, until their names and faces ran together in a beautiful, but blurred, picture. She jotted down names and phone numbers, made appointments, all while indulging in some of the best seafood she'd ever eaten. She couldn't help but notice that there were no other Boones present at the boil, besides Bael and the cousin she'd briefly met at City Hall.

What was his name again? Balfour. Balfour, whose oily charm had left her feeling like she needed a full body decontamination shower. She noted that while Bael was treated with just as much warmth and affection as anyone else, Balfour stood apart from the others, like he was contained in an invisible five-foot bubble. He wore a little smirk, watching his neighbors like they were particularly interesting specimens on a nature special. No one spoke to him. No one offered him a beer or a pat on the shoulder. He made eye contact with her over the heads of the other revelers and smiled, but not in the same friendly way everybody else was smiling. Balfour's smile sent a shiver down her spine. She turned away from him, happy to be distracted by Theresa's offer of a beer.

As night fell and the families became more comfortable, the *magique* relaxed into their true forms. Zed was so full of beer and crawfish that he curled up under a table as an enormous brown bear and fell asleep. Children ducked through the yard, chasing each other as puppies and lion cubs. The fae folk loosened their glamours like tight-fitting pants, letting green skin and sharp, mossy teeth show through. Jillian tried so hard not to stare, but the casual magic was just so fascinating to watch. They performed minor miracles as indifferently as she would pass the salt.

Some of those fae took out guitars, a harmonica, and an accordion and began playing cheerful zydeco music. A makeshift dancefloor formed on the grass and families took to dancing off their dinner. Jillian took a break once she'd had her fill of shrimp and her hand started to cramp. She wandered to a large table set with dozens of pies, beside which stood a thin, short woman with an elfin face and short gray hair. The little woman seemed none too glad to see Jillian, squinting at her so hard Jillian was afraid she might rupture something.

"Hello."

The little woman was silent, but her squint was still quite strong, reminding Jillian of childhood warnings that her own face "could freeze like that." A tall man in his late thirties with silver touching the dark hair at his temples approached, his hand outstretched.

"Simon Malfater," he said, shaking her hand enthusiastically, his deep blue eyes twinkling. "One of the rare humans here in town. I teach science at the school."

"Jillian Ramsay. Very nice to meet you."

The little woman was still squinting. An African-American man, older than Simon, with a genial smile and a big pot belly, patted Jillian's shoulder. He was wearing an LSU shirt and a pair of orange suspenders that matched the orange laces in his workboots.

"This is Siobhan," he told her, gesturing toward the tiny grumpy woman. "She's worked with Bathtilda Boone down at the pie shop ever since I was a boy. I'm Ted Beveux."

"Nice to meet you, too. Did I do something to offend her?" Jillian whispered.

Simon scoffed as Siobhan handed him a plate of pecan pie. "No, Siobhan is just trying to figure out what kind of pie to serve you."

Jillian laughed. "Oh, that's easy. I'll take a slice of lemon meringue, please."

"It's better if you let me choose for you," the little woman rumbled in a voice thick and dark as molasses.

"Isn't it traditional to let a guest choose their own food?" Jillian asked.

"It's better if you let her choose," Balfour told her, appearing at her shoulder and making Jillian jump. He always seemed to be materializing out of nowhere. It was an incredibly annoying habit-slash-skill. Balfour pulled his own fork out of his cherry pie and savored the filling from the tines in a nearly obscene manner. "Siobhan is a brownie and she has a knack for guessing this sort of thing."

Jillian pursed her lips. "Really, I'd like a slice of lemon meringue, please."

The brownie sighed as she crossed to the lemon meringue pie stand and slid a perfectly measured slice onto a small plate. "Enjoy, she muttered. "Not like I know anything. I've only been serving pie for two hundred damn years."

Jillian frowned a little while taking her first bite. It was a decent enough pie. The lemon filling was tart and smooth. The meringue was perfectly browned and then fluffy on the inside. The crust was flaky and light. But as a whole, it was just sort of...blah.

"It's better if you let her choose," Ted told her.

"I'll keep that in mind for the future," Jillian said, discreetly dumping her pie into the garbage. "So, Simon, does your family have any *magique* in its history?"

"No, we're all human," he said, picking at his pie. "Mundane as they come."

"Well, I need the human perspective for my report, too. Everybody is part of the bigger picture."

Simon smiled, his expression grateful. "How long is this report going to be? My students complain when I make them write more than five pages."

She waved her hand. "Report is actually a little misleading. This isn't going to be some brief impact summary. It's more like a book, about a hundred thousand words or so, multiple chapters, subheads, full analysis. There will be pie charts and graphs."

Simon shuddered. "That sounds terrifying."

"And yet readable enough that when we give it to community leaders, they will actually crack it open," she added, in an airy tone.

Simon threw his head back and cackled, a laugh that died down as Balfour moved closer to her.

"You've got quite the job ahead of you," Balfour noted. And while she smiled politely, Jillian didn't respond. She didn't like Balfour or the way he was glowering at Simon Malfater, trying to edge him out of the circle of conversation with body language and eye-bullying.

"So, what's it like to live here as a human?" she asked.

Simon jerked his shoulders. "It's difficult sometimes. Especially when you're a kid and everybody else is running around with special powers and all you can do is ride really fast on your bike. But I wouldn't want to live anywhere else. This is home."

"That makes sense," she assured him. "It was hard for me to leave Ohio. And there wasn't even much left for me there."

"Well, I'm a gator shifter and I'd be tickled pink to tell you all about it," Ted interjected. "Put me down for one of them appointments this week. I've got fishing to do on the weekend."

Jillian shook his hand. "I'd love that, thank you. Just write your name and number on this pad and we'll get a time set up."

Simon finished his pie and nodded toward some couples swaying on the "dancefloor" to a more somber, romantic song about a woman who drowns in her tears for a lost love.

"Would you like to dance?" he asked.

Balfour was watching her closely, she realized, in that creepy reptilian way of his. If she turned Simon down, that gave Balfour an opening to ask her and she definitely didn't want to dance with Balfour. Or touch him. Or stand too close to him, really.

Jillian glanced at Ted, who grinned and waved them off. "Go enjoy yourselves, young people."

Jillian nodded and let Simon take her hand. He felt warm and solid and utterly normal underneath the palm pressed against his starched cotton shirt. He was serviceable, like an old pair of shoes you kept around because you needed to wear *something* while you were mowing the lawn. Jillian suddenly felt sorry for this perfectly nice man, with his nice manners and his freshly pressed khakis, who had to compete with the likes of Zed and Bael for female attention. She imagined Mystic Bayou's dating pool was a pretty savage ecosystem.

"You know, I've taken some measurements of electromagnetic fields and currents near the rift if you want to look at them sometime," he offered shyly.

And even though she would have to take her own measurements of the rift to assure accuracy, she smiled and said, "That would be so helpful, thank you."

Because a man of science should feel like he had a chance, even when competing with were-bears and...whatever the hell Bael was.

"I'd like to visit the site itself as soon as I can get Zed or someone to lead me. There's a lot of concern about me getting lost in the swamp."

"I could take you," Simon offered, but suddenly his hold on her waist loosened and he stepped back from her. She frowned and glanced over her shoulder to find Bael staring down at the teacher.

"Simon," Bael purred. "You wouldn't mind if I borrowed Miss Jillian here for a dance, would you?"

Simon's mouth worked open and shut like a trout, but he produced no response. Bael wrapped his hot fingers around her wrist and led her away. Though she was sad to leave Simon behind, her shoulders relaxed more and more the farther she got from Balfour.

"It's Dr. Ramsay," she reminded him lightly, noting that the makeshift band was playing a slow, sad song about a boy who fell in love with the moon. "And I don't remember saying yes to a dance."

"I know, I just like how pissed off you get when I don't get it right," he shot back. "And you're going to dance with me because you know you want to. And because I'm a better dancer than Simon. He's all elbows and smashed toes."

Bael's hand slid across her back, leaving a trail of heat across her skin, even through her shirt. She should have found it uncomfortable, considering the humidity and the disdain he'd shown her at every step, but she was leaning into him. Hell, she was barely restraining the urge to lay her forehead against his chest, the scent of bonfire smoke and warm summer spices luring her closer. He clutched her fingers in his other hand, pressing it to his chest as they circled in box-steps to the music.

She looked up, her nose dangerously close to brushing against his jaw. "You didn't have to be so rude to Mr. Malfater. He seems like a perfectly nice man."

"You say that 'cause you didn't see what he did to his prom date's feet. Besides, maybe I don't want you dancing with perfectly nice men. Or Zed."

Jillian laughed. "Oh, I should be dancing with you instead?"

He nodded. "Yes."

"Ha, so you admit that you're not nice."

Bael pretended to be wounded for a second. "I'm the soul of kindness."

"You're a pain in my ass."

Bael shrugged. "Never said different. So, other than ridin' on

Zed's bike and dancing with the world's blandest man, how's your evening going?"

"Really, well!" she said, brightly, just to torture him. "I persuaded the editor of the Mystic Messenger to let me put a survey insert into Wednesday's paper. And I have ten interviews scheduled in the next week. I'll give you a copy of my schedule so you can babysit me. I have a few interviews scheduled under Zed's supervision at City Hall on Monday morning. And then I'm supposed to visit Ted Beveux's place on Tuesday afternoon."

While she'd made the baby-sitting comment to needle at him, she didn't expect his face to darken the way it did. He insisted, "You don't want to interview him."

"Why not? He's an alligator shifter, which is really rare. And he's not a pervert, which means he's a safer choice than the Beasleys."

"What about Stu Moffatt? He's a pooka," Bael said. "They're a dying breed. Or Dickon Macey? He seems a little hurt you haven't asked him yet. He said y'all had a real nice conversation at the gas station the other day. Or Theresa?"

"I've already scheduled an interview with Theresa. Why don't you want me to interview Ted?" she asked.

Bael refused to meet her eyes, staring over the top of her head. But his voice, it wasn't the usual forthright timbre she'd become accustomed to, but the reedy, higher notes of a lie. "I just think you'd be better off devoting your time to other people."

Jillian frowned. "Well, maybe it's none of your business who I interview."

"Is every conversation we have going to end up like this?" he demanded, finally looking at her again.

"Probably."

He huffed and puffed, but pinched the bridge of his thin nose and laughed.

"I noticed that your accent's not as thick as some of your

neighbors. And you don't use as many of the idioms. The interesting little Cajun sayings, which is a shame because I actually find them pretty charming."

Bael shrugged, the motion carrying the hand at her back to mess up her hair. He smoothed it against her back, and slipped his hand down her spine, ever so slightly below her waistline and then right back up to respectable territory. "My family has always held themselves apart from the rest of the creatures here. We don't trust or make friends easily. So, we held on to our natural accent longer."

"And where did the natural accent come from?"

"The North," he said.

Jillian lowered her voice. "You may not have heard this before, but a lot of places have a north."

Now it was his turn to smirk. "Yes, you're right."

"You're going to be very difficult to interview," she said, squinting at him.

"I don't plan on letting you interview me."

"Fine, I'll just distill what I can from your scintillating conversational skills," she muttered.

Bael nodded at the people around them, enjoying themselves so thoroughly. "This was a warm reception for you."

"Yes, it's nice to be welcomed like this into the community," she conceded. "I know that's not always the case with League representatives."

"Just keep in mind that Zed was careful to only invite people who were happy you're here. This isn't a fair representation of local opinion."

"Why do you always have to do that?" she hissed, pulling out of his arms. "Why do you always have to remind me that I'm not wanted here, even if it's just by you? That you don't support what I'm doing? Why can't you just let it rest for a night?"

"Because I don't want you to drop your guard. I want you to stay safe," he insisted.

"You want me to stay uncomfortable," she told him.

"If that's what keeps you safe, then yes."

She stepped away from him, keeping her voice low to avoid making a scene at Clarissa's party. "Every time I think I'm on the verge of understanding you or at least being able to work with you, you do...this. Do me a favor. Forget about my guard. Just stay away from me. And keep your opinions to yourself."

With that, she disappeared into the crowd to find Zed and get a ride home.

7

JILLIAN

Jillian climbed out of the van and checked her bag to make sure she had the right pens to color code her notes—because that was her level of compulsion.

"*How* is a fun-loving girl like you single?" she muttered.

This was her ninth interview of the week, including the local postmaster (a touch-know psychic), the school principal (a werewolf), the local funeral director (a human), the proprietor of a catfish farm (a river nymph) and Zed's mother, Clarissa. Zed's presence during her interviews was about as helpful as a paper oven mitt, but it seemed to make the subjects feel comfortable to have him there.

She was gathering great information, and an outline was already forming in her head in terms of how she was going to organize it.

This afternoon, she'd defied logic and Bael's instructions, using her GPS and a map to find a route to Ted Beveux's house. It only took her an hour and a half to complete what should have been a fifteen-mile trip.

She would never tell a soul.

She hadn't spoken to Bael since the ill-fated crawfish boil dance. Whenever their paths crossed at City Hall, she managed to avoid eye contact and dash into Zed's office. She was more hurt by Bael's behavior than she expected. She didn't know why it mattered so much that he didn't support her efforts in Mystic Bayou. She only knew that even four days later, it still made her stomach turn to hear his voice. Zed seemed confused by her refusal to talk to Bael, but was smart enough not to talk about it or try to force a reconciliation.

But now, she branched out to interviewing subjects in their homes without supervision. Ted said that he couldn't make it into town because he was preparing for a big annual fishing trip. Ted's house was a bit more in line with what she'd expected. While the boat tied off to Ted's backyard dock, the *St. Marie,* was in excellent condition, the house had seen better days. It desperately needed a new coat of yellow paint and the stilts seemed to be crumbling beneath it. She could smell the rot of damp wood and mildew from the driveway. And something else, maybe old fish? Crab pots and netting hung neatly arranged on a fence just beside the house. She'd read somewhere that gator hunters sometimes used rotten meat for bait because the alligators like it better. Maybe Ted was curing some bait?

The smell grew stronger as she got closer to the house. From inside the screen door, she could hear an intense buzzing, as if Ted was using an electric shaver. Jillian appreciated that he wanted to get cleaned up for her, but clearing the house of rotted meat was probably a better first step.

She's knocked gingerly on the rusty screen door. "Mr. Beveux? It's Jillian Ramsay. We have an appointment today? Hello?"

Silence. Well, not silence. She could still hear the buzzing of the electric shaver.

"Mr. Beveux?"

When no one answered, she walked along the wraparound porch connected to the dock, circling toward the back of the house. At first, all her brain processed was the pretty set-up, a wide porch swing and a dock that dropped straight into the water without the obstruction of a railing. Then her eyes landed on a crumpled red heap near the back door, a shiny wet mess covered in writhing black.

Then she realized, the buzzing wasn't a razor. It was flies.

"What?" she gasped, pressing her hand to her mouth and turning away from the sight of the carcass. And that's when she remembered, Ted was a gator shifter. He wouldn't be curing gator bait because he wouldn't hunt gators. Had Ted butchered an animal back here? He didn't seem like the type to just leave a carcass on his own back porch. Especially not when he was expecting company.

"Ted!" she yelled, barely holding down the breakfast she'd eaten that morning.

She pulled out her phone, her sweaty fingers slipping over the glass surface as she tried to enter her security code. She stepped a little closer to the mess of torn flesh and recognized Ted's boots with the orange laces. The mess was wearing Ted's boots. And what used to be blue jeans.

The mess was Ted.

Jillian ran to the edge of the porch, dropped to her knees and threw up into the water. Her world was reduced to the blood roaring through her ears and the panic purging from her stomach. She collapsed against the rough wood, barely escaping a face-first tumble into the water. She rolled onto her back, breathing heavily and praying she wouldn't throw up again. She took a few deep gasping breaths and then remembered the gators who occupied the swamp, gators that had probably killed Ted. She scooted a little farther away from the edge of the dock.

She finally managed to unlock her phone, only to find that

she didn't have any bars. She walked into Ted's open kitchen door, careful to keep her eyes off of the body, and found his landline phone. She dialed City Hall's number, wondering why she bothered carrying her cell phone at all, beyond a sense of "security."

Theresa Anastas's calm, accented voice sounded in her ear and she nearly wept with relief. "Theresa, this is Jillian Ramsay. We met at Clarissa's crawfish boil the other night? Could you please tell the sheriff to meet me at Ted Beveux's place? There's an emergency."

"Sure thing, Jillian. Are you OK?" Theresa asked.

Jillian was shaking her head for several moments before she realized that Theresa couldn't hear her. "No."

Jillian spent the next ten minutes looking out at the water and doing deep breathing exercises, intentionally looking away from poor Ted's body. She had no idea how to handle this situation. No one had ever explained how to behave when you showed up for an interview and found the subject torn to shreds. What had happened? Shouldn't gators avoid a gator shifter out of respect? What sort of animal could leave a person in that condition? Was the animal still close by?

She moved away from the edge of the dock, until her back was resting against the house. She slid up the wall to a standing position. Maybe she should just leave and let Bael take care of this. It was his job, not hers. She was a scientist, not a cop. But then, she glanced at Ted's blood-soaked boots with their silly orange laces, and she knew she couldn't leave him alone like this.

"Jillian?"

She looked up to see Bael standing at the corner of the porch, gun drawn.

Bael holstered his gun, his expression grim. She crossed the porch in three steps, and threw her arms around his neck and sobbed into his throat. Bael's arms slowly circled her body.

Tucking her head under his chin, he murmured soft words in a language she didn't understand. She didn't realize she was crying until his wet uniform shirt stuck to her cheek. He was so warm and that was a blissful contrast to her cold, clammy skin.

"It's all right," he whispered against her temple. "You're all right. You're safe. I've got you."

He rubbed his hands over her hair, down her spine. She let herself bask in his comfort for just a few more seconds, before peeling herself away. He cupped her chin in his hands and then placed a Taser between her shaking palms. "You stay here. You hear anything, call Zed."

Bael walked inside the house and was gone for several minutes. She listened carefully, but she couldn't even hear his footsteps as he moved around on the ancient floorboards. He was holstering his gun again as he walked back out.

"The house is clear."

"I didn't think to check further in the house," she admitted.

"You're very lucky there was nobody inside. What if whatever did this to Ted came out and hurt you?"

"Well the next time I find a dead body, I'll be sure to check the perimeter," she said, the tiniest bit of sass returning to her voice.

He glared at her, but there was no real heat in it. "I've got to go to my car to radio for Zed. Do you want to sit here or go with me?"

She shook her head. "I don't think my legs will work just yet. You go on."

A few minutes later, Bael returned with a cold bottle of water and a bottle of whiskey. "Which one do you want?"

She took the bottle of water and gulped down most of it in one go. His eyebrows shot up when she took the whiskey bottle and drank a good portion of it, too.

Bael blinked rapidly. "Damn."

She glared up at him.

"What time did you get here?" he asked, taking out his notebook.

"Just a few minutes before I called Theresa," she said, sipping more water and wiping her mouth with the back of her hand. "We had an appointment today. He didn't answer my knock at the front door so I came around back and I found him like this."

She glanced over to the body, and swallowed heavily as the whiskey threatened to come back up. Bael clasped her shoulder. "Don't look at him. You've done all you can for him. Look at me."

She looked up into his face and for the first time, found his expression to be completely free of suspicion or irritation. It was a face she could spend a lot of time admiring, if it could stay that way. "What do you think could've done this?"

"I'm not so sure it's a what. I'm thinking it's a who."

At her confused expression, he continued. "It's probably hard to tell from that distance and with this much blood. But Ted wasn't clawed. He wasn't bitten. You probably couldn't see close enough, but those are cuts made with a very sharp knife. See there? Even his jeans have been cut off, with surgical scissors maybe."

"I had no interest in getting closer to the body to get a better look."

Bael swiped his hand over his head. "I don't blame you. I'm not real happy about it myself."

"So if this wasn't an animal, who would do this to Ted? Did he have any problems with anyone in town?"

Bael jerked his shoulders. "Not that I can think of. Ted pretty much got along with everybody. I can name at least ten guys I'd guess would be murdered before Ted."

"You keep lists like that in your head?"

And when Bael didn't answer, Jillian asked, "Who will you even call about this? You don't have a town doctor. You can't exactly call in the medical examiner from the next parish to examine a shifter body."

"I really don't know," he admitted. "We haven't had a murder in this town in decades. I'm a one-man department. I don't have a coroner. We have a funeral home, but poor David Wyatt isn't prepared to gather evidence for something like this."

"I think there's a forensic science department at the League offices. You can always send pictures to them to see if they can interpret the wounds."

He nodded. "We'll see. For now, why don't you just head on home? You don't need to be here for this. I'll come by your place later to ask some more questions."

"I don't want to leave you alone," she said. "What if the killer comes back?"

"You're gonna protect little ol' me?" he asked, smirking slightly as he slid his hand through her hair and cupped the back of her head.

"OK, what if the killer is watching us right now and follows me home?"

Bael frowned. "Good point. Stay right here."

She'd expected Bael to leave her alone on the porch while he went through Ted's house. But he stood by her side, keeping her distracted with inane questions about how she'd found her way to the house and who else she had scheduled to interview that week. Though she was somewhat calmer with Bael beside her, she still jerked slightly when she heard Zed's motorcycle roll up. His boots were heavy against the porch as he jogged around the corner. He didn't even pause as he dropped a large rucksack, sped past Bael and yanked her off of her feet into a bear hug.

"Are you OK?" he demanded, crushing her against his barrel chest.

Her hands batted weakly against the ponytail trailing down his back. "Oxygen."

"Oh, right, sorry." Zed placed her back on her feet and put his hand on top of her head while checking her over. "But you're OK?"

"I'm fine," she promised. "But poor Ted."

Zed nodded. "Bael, what can I do?"

For the next hour, Zed and Jillian helped Bael document the crime scene. Jillian used her camera to take photos of the body and the position of items around him. Zed videotaped the interior of the house and used baggies from Ted's kitchen to bag evidence. Zed recorded observations on a mini-recorder.

"Is this really legal? Chain of custody-wise?" she asked.

Zed pursed his lips and grabbed a nearby book. He placed Jillian's hand on it and raised his hand. "Jillian Ramsay, I hereby deputize you as a law enforcement official in the Mystic Parish. Do you swear to follow Sheriff Bael Boone's orders and uphold the law to the best of your ability?"

"This is a copy of *The Da Vinci Code*," she noted.

"Do you swear?"

"Define 'follow orders,' because I don't want to accidentally enter into some sort of sex contract with Bael." She jerked her thumb toward the sheriff, who bobbled the measuring tape he was holding and dropped it on Ted's chest.

Zed frowned. "You OK, buddy?"

Bael waved them off and wandered toward the end of the dock. "Yeah, I'm just going to go measure something...over there."

Zed winked at her. "That was kind of mean, but I'm glad your sense of humor is coming back to you."

"I swear, I will not contaminate evidence or break the law and will follow orders where I see fit," she said, then returned the book to its original position.

Nothing in the house explained why someone would want to hurt Ted, no weird collections of women's undergarments in marked bags, no hate mail, no piles of drugs or cash marked "ill-gotten gains." He was just a nice, normal man, living alone in the swamp with an enormous backlog of crushed beer cans—who happened to be able to turn into an alligator but that seemed superfluous to how he died.

But Jillian finally got it. As Zed took a sheet from his rucksack and gently laid it over Ted's body, Jillian understood why the people of Mystic Bayou elected Zed to lead them. In a crisis, Zed was the guy to have around, focused and patient and detail-oriented. He didn't question Bael's decisions. He made helpful suggestions. He didn't smirk once.

She hated the way she startled when she heard another vehicle pull into the driveway. Was this the way it was going to be every time a vehicle approached for the rest of her life? Or was "finding a dead body" PTSD a two- or three-week thing?

She bolted through the house to where they were standing, near Ted's covered body. "Did you two call someone else? A car just came up the driveway."

"I asked my *maman* to come take you home," Zed told her. "I can load my bike in her truck and drive it home."

"I think I can drive myself. I managed to find my way here. After a while," she said.

"After we told you not to." Bael called from across the dock.

"I don't like the idea of you stayin' out at Miss Lottie's by yourself," Zed told her.

"I'm sure I'll be fine. I don't think whoever did this to Ted is going to go to Lottie's house just because I happened to find him," she insisted.

"It's actually not a terrible idea," Bael added. "We haven't had a murder in decades. You come to town and we have a murder? It tracks that they could be connected."

"Are you saying this is my fault?"

Before Bael could respond, Zed jerked those broad shoulders

of his. "You can stay at my place if you want. It's probably the safest den in the parish."

"No," Bael barked sharply.

Jillian and Zed whipped their heads toward Bael, whose cheeks went pink. "Because uh, you just turned your guest room into a sports cave."

"I could sleep on the couch," Zed said, shrugging.

Bael's scowl was a thing of thunderous beauty.

"I'll be fine. I'll lock my doors. I'll take your Taser with me if it will make you feel better."

Bael shook his head. "I don't think it would."

8

BAEL

In the south, the local breakfast place was the hub of all morning conversation and gossip. It was the grease-soaked equivalent of the watering hole on a nature special.

The pie shop was a pre-Civil War wood structure with a pressed tin roof and walls painted white and emerald green. All of the art on the walls featured gold foil in some capacity, whether it was a landscape, a painting of the kitten, an old icon of an orthodox saint. The mismatched paintings added a sort of quirky whimsy to the old-fashioned diner set up, with the long-polished wood lunch counter and weathered booths. True to its name, at least a dozen clear glass pie stands stood on the counter displaying different types of pie.

Normally, Bael found comfort in this community and familiarity, in enjoying his morning pie with his neighbors. But this morning, he could find no crust-based solace.

It had been a very long week for Bael: informing Ted's family of his death, helping them arrange the funeral, containing the details of the case like a virus, as not to inspire panic. Fortunately, the Beveuxs had agreed that it was better to let people think Ted had an accident that required a close-casket service. They knew that it wouldn't benefit the community to be afraid.

The only contact Bael'd had with Jillian was when she'd helped him send photos and evidence to the League's forensics department, who didn't want to give a full analysis just yet, but were willing to say, "Yeah, an animal didn't do that." He was paraphrasing, of course, but hoped to get a little more information out of Jillian's coworkers that might actually help him figure out what had befallen poor Ted.

How had something like this happened in his town? They hadn't had a murder in years, decades even, and that had been some old country feud between two recently transplanted Romanian werewolves. Who would want to kill Ted Beveux in such a bloody, vicious manner?

Bael scanned the room, full of people he'd known since he was a boy, and he couldn't imagine a single one of them hurting someone that badly. The idea that someone he knew could have done this, left him...disappointed. He thought he knew these people. The previous week, he would have told Jillian that this was one of the safest places in the world for *magique* and humans alike. And now, they had a murderer in their midst.

It had to be a local. Ted rarely had contact with anyone outside of Mystic Bayou, and he doubted an outsider could have found Ted's house. Jillian only found it because she was one of the most disturbingly tenacious people he'd ever met.

Jillian. It surprised him that he felt oddly bereft without seeing her all week. He missed her constant curiosity and her scent and the way she was sickeningly sweet to everybody but him. He wondered why she seemed to be hiding out in Miss Lottie's house. Surely, she had to have run through the groceries they'd left for her. But Zed had assured Bael that Jillian was fine, she was just busy working. And then Zed gave him shit for asking about her.

She was a human. She was a *nosy* human whom he wanted to vacate from Mystic Bayou as soon as possible. She checked off every single box on his list labeled, "DO NOT WANT." And yet, it was taking all of his will power to stay in his seat and not drive out to Miss Lottie's to check on her. He could get past this, he told himself. He could ignore Jillian Ramsay.

Now, Jillian Ramsay was walking through the pie shop's door.

Dammit.

As she closed the door behind her, the drone of conversation faded to silence. Bael glanced around. That wasn't good. For that many people to stop talking all at once, meant that most of them had been talking about her. And not in a "she's such a lovely girl who was raised right" sort of way. From his corner booth where no one dared join him, Balfour smirked and it was all Bael could do not to throw a cake stand across the room at him.

For her part, Jillian simply smiled and walked across the room as casually as she could. She took a seat next to Bael at the counter. "Good morning."

"Morning," he muttered, lifting his coffee cup to his lips.

"So, that was awkward."

"Yes, it was."

"So that was the international signal for 'We're talking about you right before you walked in.' What gives? Do they think I had something to do with hurting Ted?"

He frowned at her. "You didn't come to the funeral."

"Of course I didn't. I barely knew Ted. I didn't want to intrude or be a distraction."

"I thought you were supposed to be documenting local traditions. Funerals are a big tradition around here," he told her.

Jillian shifted, clearly uncomfortable. "I didn't think it was my place. I didn't know whether Ted's family would be uncomfortable with me being there, considering I'm the one who found him. And I thought it might come across as ghoulish. Like I was trying to turn their pain into fodder for my study. I was trying to *avoid* hurting feelings, not cause them."

He felt an unexpected rush of warmth toward her. She was trying to do the right thing, and had misstepped, which was easy to do when she was so far outside her comfort zone. And she seemed genuinely upset that she might have hurt the Beveuxs' feelings.

"It will blow over," he assured her. "Just take the Beveuxs a casserole and a nice card, let them know you're thinking of them and explain your reasons for skipping the funeral, just like you explained them to me. It will go a long way."

She pulled a face. "A casserole? That would require cooking, wouldn't it?"

"Ask Miss Clarissa for help."

"Can't I just take one of these pies?" she asked, jerking in alarm when Siobhan appeared behind the counter from nowhere. And Siobhan was squinting at her again—while pouring Jillian a cup of coffee, which upped the degree of squinting difficulty considerably.

"Is this facial expression because I didn't let you choose my pie?" Jillian asked.

"It's better if you let me choose."

Bael nodded. "It's better if you let her choose."

Jillian grumbled, "Fine, fine, choose a pie for me, please."

Siobhan slipped away to choose from the domes of pie.

Jillian turned to him. "Isn't it kind of early for pie?"

"Don't ever let Siobhan hear you say that," Bael told her. "Pie is considered an all-day food around here. Siobhan bakes a little bit of magic into every one of them. Pies to soothe your temper. Pies to settle a troubled soul. Pies to spark your passions."

Jillian shook her head. "It's pie."

"I will take your coffee if you keep talking this way." He grabbed for her cup, and she was quick enough to snatch it away and cradle it to her chest without spilling a drop. The grin he gave her was downright predatory. Her brows drew down, an open challenge.

Siobhan broke the tension, serving Jillian a slice of a pie with a chocolate filling and what looked like chunks of red fruit.

"Chocolate rhubarb, house specialty." Siobhan gave her a sharp nod and walked away. Jillian's mouth turned downward in a pout that made Bael want to bite her lip.

Jillian tried to subtly sniff at the plate. "I've never had chocolate rhubarb pie before. I don't think I've even had rhubarb before."

Bael handed her a fork. "Trust me."

Jillian took a bite and gave an indecent moan. Bael squirmed on his barstool, strategically dropping a napkin over his lap. She licked her fork, which was not helping Bael's napkin situation. "This is magic. Sweet and dark with just a little bit of sour. Like a dessert wine in a crust."

Bael cleared his throat. "See?"

"It's better if I let her choose," she said, nodding.

"I told you!" Siobhan called from across the shop.

"I thought Bathtilda Boone owned this shop," Jillian noted.

"She does. But the woman could burn water. She's the brains behind the operation, not the cook. She found Siobhan right after my family crossed the ocean. Brownies are rare here, without anyone who knows to leave milk out for them or reward their little courtesies. And Siobhan rewarded Bathtilde for her protection by suggesting they open the shop. So why are you here, intruding on my morning pie?" Bael asked as Jillian dug into her "breakfast."

"I have questions."

Bael snorted into his own coffee cup. "What else is new?"

"It's about the rift."

Bael set down his coffee cup and frowned at her. "What about it?"

"I was looking at some of the census records Zed gave me, and I'm finding families that don't make sense. *Magique* being born in families where there's never been a *magie* before. Humans who have no magic or fae in their family line, suddenly developing power over water or weather. I don't have to tell you, that's not the way it works. Shifters are born, not bitten."

"Stop," he said quietly, glancing around the restaurant to see if anyone was listening.

But Jillian's stream of consciousness could not be dammed. "And the only thing I can think of that would make the difference is the rift. Does the rift affect people here? The humans? Hell, the *magique*? Does it change how they transform? That much energy has to have some sort of side effect, right? Like a supernatural cancer cluster?"

"Stop."

Jillian shrugged. "What? I'm just asking. Surely people around here have to know about it."

"Stop, now," he said, taking her arm and pulling her out of her seat. He picked up her hideous bag and slung it over his shoulder, leading her outside of the shop and across the street.

Balfour yelled from the back of the pie shop, "When you get tired of her, Bael, you give me a call!"

Bael ignored his cousin and the ripple of uncomfortable laughter that followed them out the door. He was well-aware that by the end of the day, a story would be circulating on the kitchen circuit that Bael and Jillian had a lovers' quarrel in the pie shop and he dragged her outside to prevent her from blabbing all of his sex secrets to onlookers. And Zed would be responsible for spreading most of that story, because he was a gossipy dick.

"What was that about?" she grunted, jerking her arm out of his grip.

"You can't ask those questions in the pie shop where anybody can hear you." He was leaning too close, he knew, towering over her so their conversation couldn't be heard by passersby. It was as maddening as it was fascinating that even as he boxed her in, she didn't back down. She just set her jaw in that mulish, stubborn line and stared him right in the eye.

"This is just great. By the time the rumor mill stops grinding, everybody in town will think I'm knocked up with two or three of your young."

He sniffed. "Impossible, human women can only carry one of our eggs at a time."

Her dark blue eyes narrowed at him. "Beg pardon?"

"Look, everything you just mentioned? You can't bring it up in your report."

"Why?" she exclaimed. "If it has something to do with how well your town has integrated, it should be in the report. It could help people."

"It can't help anyone else," he insisted. "And it can only hurt us."

She inhaled deeply through her nose and closed her eyes, which he'd come to understand was her "praying for patience" face. She asked him, "Please explain what you mean."

He pulled her a bit more gently toward the gazebo in the center of the town square. They passed a plaque commemorating the founding of the town and climbed its worn steps. The large white-washed structure was flanked by benches on all sides and featured a large swing, big enough to seat five or six people.

"Sit," he told her, scanning the surrounding area for other

people. And when he saw the rigid set of her chin, he added, "Please."

When she sat, with little grace, he said, "Part of the reason we're drawn here is there's a concentration of energy out in the center of the swamp. It pulls us, makes us feel safe. It's why we settled here."

"Yes, I researched it pretty thoroughly," she said, her tone dry.

"Well, what you don't know is that the rift is destabilizing. Over the last few decades, creatures are being born to human families, without any let's say interference from the supernatural families."

"Are you sure it's just not a case of couples not wanting to admit that they messed around?" she asked.

"We're sure. We had a *mohana* born to a human family last year. We never had a *mohana* family here," he said.

Jillian's eyes brightened. "Oh! I can help with that. I've actually done a lot of research on *mohanas*. I was called away for a research trip on a group of *mohanas* in Chile, to come here. If the family has any questions I'd be happy to help."

"You really know how to find the silver lining in a situation, don't you?" Bael deadpanned.

"I regret nothing."

"Well, the family wasn't nearly as enthusiastic as you—" His head cocked to the side as he pulled a confused face. "The League was doing an in-depth study of hyper-sexual dolphin shifters?"

"They're one of the more obscure shifter cultures, and awfully reclusive when it comes to academia," she said with a shrug. "It was a bit of a coup to secure an invitation."

He snorted. "Don't worry, sweetheart, we'll get you back to your creeper dolphin soon enough."

"How many of these, let's call them 'remade' *magique* have

been created over the years?" she asked, relaxing a bit into the swing, pushing off with her feet.

"I'd say thirty or so over the years. But the real problem is humans who were born human taking on supernatural qualities in their later years. Ted Beveux only started shifting into an alligator about ten years ago. His entire line is human, as far as we know. Gladys Fider was as human as you get until about two years ago, and now all of a sudden, she sprouts porcupine quills when she gets mad. Teenie Clackston went from a regular empty-nester housewife to a full-on kitchen witch. Best damn blackberry wine I ever tasted. Hell, the Honey Island swamp monster was actually one of our local fishermen, Xavier Ronson. Fifty years ago, he woke up on a camping trip covered in fur. 'Course, he freaked out, running out of his tent and onto a road where he scared some wildlife photographer and the legend was born. He was our first. But his mother was distantly related to Zed's family and we thought maybe it was just recessive genes popping up. It started off slowly, so sparse we thought it was a freak occurrence, but now it's happening every year."

She frowned as she pushed off the floor of the gazebo to swing. "But that doesn't make any sense. Why would that start suddenly after years of living around the rift with no problem?"

"We don't know, either. And it's not exactly a problem we want to advertise. Every whacklaloon from here to Canada would be at our doors, wanting to be exposed to the rift so they can become a *magie*. Not to mention it could expose our secret to the human world at large. This is why I didn't want you interviewing Ted the other day. I was hoping I could steer you away from the 'remade' shifters, to keep you from finding out about the rift's effects. But clearly, that was a mistake, because you're like a badger when it comes to information you're not supposed to have."

"You may think that's an insult, but it's not," she sniffed.

Bael rolled his eyes.

Jillian asked, "Why didn't you tell the League about this?"

"We weren't sure how it would affect us getting the League's help and we need the money. We didn't want them deciding that we weren't fit for the study because we have anomalies."

Jillian's mouth dropped open, forming a surprised little "o." "What money?"

"In exchange for participating in the study, they're giving the town money and medical support we need pretty desperately," he told her. "We haven't had a town doctor in five years and not all of our citizens can go to the ER when they have medical problems."

Jillian gasped. "But that's unethical. It creates pressure on the subjects to comply and could lead to inappropriate or even falsified responses to keep the League happy."

"Really, you're shocked that the League is behaving in a less than absolutely pristine ethical manner? Have you ever dealt with the League before? The same people who threatened all *magique* creatures with extinction if we didn't agree to the Pact of Secrecy in 1800? The same people who threatened us with extinction if we didn't agree to a regular census in 1908?"

"But that was more than a hundred years ago," she protested.

He didn't mean to tilt his head and look at her like she was an adorable *imbecile*, but honestly. "The same creatures who were in charge of the League a hundred years ago are in charge of the League now, Jillian. It's one of the benefits of being a *magie*. We live longer than you."

Jillian asked, "Instead of forcing the town to rely on the League, couldn't the Boones spread their wealth around a little bit?"

He frowned at her. "It's not in our nature to 'spread our wealth around.' My family already helps in some areas that offer them some return on the investment, like providing faster Wi-Fi infrastructure for the town, which the citizens pay a monthly fee for. It wouldn't do for the town to be any more indebted to my family. It would disrupt what is already a pretty delicate balance of power."

"So it's better to indebt them to people who have threatened to mass murder you?"

"Better the devil that's far away than the devil who lives in your backyard?" he guessed.

She sighed and sagged against the rope suspending the swing. "I'm sorry."

"Not your fault. But you see now, why I get a little agitated, talking about your study."

She nodded. "When does that doctor get here?"

"In a few months, after we make a good show of participating in the study."

"I want to see it," she said, firmly.

"The doctor? Not very nice to call him an 'it.'"

She kicked off the floor and swung, nearly kicking him in the shin. "The rift."

"You can't."

"Because it's invisible?" she asked.

He lifted an eyebrow. "No, because everybody who tries to get too close to it ends up passing out and sleeping for about six months until they heal from the internal trauma caused by random barometric pressure spikes. The closest we *magique* can get to it is about three hundred yards. Humans? Five hundred or so. Just close enough to see it through high-end binoculars."

"I'd still like to see it, document the area around it. Note how it changes the environment. What effects it has on you."

"I mentioned the six-month coma, right?"

She grinned at him. "Come on, be a buddy. If you pass out, I'll carry you back to town!"

Bael stopped her mid-swing, lifted her arm, examined her bicep and made a skeptical face.

"I would go get Zed and he would carry you back to town," she conceded.

"If I say no, you'll just go out there on your own, won't you?"

"There's a very strong possibility of that, yes."

9

JILLIAN

Hours later, she was wearing her sturdiest boots and thick canvas field pants, wading through waist-deep ferns along the edge of the "Afarpiece Swamp." It was so-named because the trek of marshland was so remote that the only way locals referred to it was saying that it was "A far piece away."

Bael didn't seem to be struggling with the vegetation like she did. He was slipping between the fronds, barely moving them, keeping a sharp eye out for the animals that seemed to be calling from every corner of the swamp.

She thought she'd been primed for the hike, because after all, she lived on the swamp in her little *maison de fous*. She carefully packed a day bag with water and sunscreen, bug spray and camera equipment.

She'd had no clue. She was not prepared for the way she could smell the heat, wet and earthen, like rotting leaves. She wasn't prepared for the way the humidity absorbed into her clothes, sealing them to her skin in a thick layer of sweat. She was not prepared for the distraction Bael's ass would pose, bobbing through the brush ahead of her like a perfect peach wrapped in skin-tight denim.

She was staring at it, suffering the oddest craving for peach pie, when he called over his shoulder, "You all right back there?"

"Are you really taking me to see the rift or is this some sort of horrible backwoods prank?" she asked.

"No, you wanted to see it," he told her. "And you're going to see it. Because I know you and if I don't help you, you'd just come out here by yourself, fall in a sinkhole and then I'd have to fish you back out. This way, I save time."

"Well, I appreciate your commitment to efficiency."

Despite the aches in her shoulders from her pack, she noted that her legs and feet didn't hurt. The moss created a thick, soft carpet beneath her boots. In fact, everything seemed to grow thick here, and super-sized. The honeysuckle climbing up the trees dripped with blossoms the size of her fist. The scent was alluring, for the first few seconds, and then it was cloying to the point that she felt like she was choking on it.

"Everything seems to be growing...more out here," she said. "Is that a normal swamp thing or a rift thing?"

"It's a rift thing. You can see the effects all over town, though. You should see the gardens we get in the fall. Pumpkins the size of a playhouse. The only problem is the kudzu."

She frowned. "Well, kudzu's a problem all over the south."

"Yeah, but our kudzu seems to be growing toward town like it's personal."

Jillian nearly tripped over a stone hidden under the fern fronds. She nudged at it with her foot and found that it was part of a line of moss-covered stones that stretched as far as she could see.

"That's the human line," he told her, catching her arm and righting her onto her feet. "This is as close as humans should get to the rift. Stay on that side of the stones."

She nodded, peering over the water, into shaded trees. "I don't see anything."

"And you're not going to from this distance." He handed her a pair of binoculars from her pack. "Wait for your eyes to adjust. It's not gonna be as dramatic as you think."

She lifted the glasses to her eyes and stared. For a few long silent moments, she saw nothing and she thought maybe Bael was pulling a joke on her after all. But then she noticed a tiny movement over the water, between the trees. He was right. There was no light or dark, no crackle of electrical light. It was a ripple, like the haze of heat over asphalt in summer.

"Wow," she sighed, moving closer, barely feeling the stones bumping her feet.

She pulled out her camera and connected the long-distance lens. She put the viewfinder to her eye and focused on the ripple, firing off several shots. She was sure it would come off like out-of-focus pictures of tree branches, but she had to at least try. She switched to an infrared camera to record the wavelength shifts in complicated color patterns. On the monitor, it looked like a rainbow was having a seizure.

She glanced from the monitor to the rift and back again. The longer she stared at it, the more she could see it move, the more she saw the patterns in its dance, like it was trying to tell her something. She reached her hand out, as if she could touch it, and she could feel *intent* from the rift. She could feel what it wanted and it wanted—

Everything went dark.

Her head drooped and she couldn't seem to control any of her muscles. She felt her body drop toward the ground like a puppet whose strings had been cut. Her jaw ached and her stomach felt like it was filled with stones. An arm slipped under her back, breaking her fall just before her head hit the stone circle.

She could feel her feet dragging over the ground as Bael moved her farther back from the stone line. Her eyes fluttered open. Bael's face swam over hers, an expression of concern furrowing his brow. She weakly lifted her hand to try to trace the lines of his cheekbones with her fingers.

"That's the rift pullin' at you," he told her, sliding his free hand under the base of her skull. "We need to get you out of here."

She nodded and immediately regretted it. It felt like her ears were going to explode. Thunderclouds rolled over Bael's head. Something cold splattered against her forehead. Bael's thumb stroked it away and he righted her onto her feet.

The cypress limbs whipped back and forth like an octopus possessed. The sky opened up and great howling sheets of water poured forth by the bucketful. Lightning sliced through a tree far too close to them and her fingers twisted into Bael's t-shirt sleeves to pull him closer. Thunder rattled through her chest and the pressure on her chest was so great, she was afraid she might pass out again. No, she had to keep going.

Shaking it off, she started to run, with Bael close behind her.

"I thought you were supposed to be able to see hurricanes from far off?" she yelled over the chaos. She reached out blindly to try to avoid running into trees. And in reaching out, she felt Bael's hand warm and solid close around her wrists. He pulled her to a stop, and panic made way for relief. She wasn't alone. She had Bael, and for all his blustering, he would not leave her alone in this.

"Not around here. The weather works differently, because of the rift. You get ten miles out of town, you probably won't even feel this. The closer we get to the rift, the more unstable the weather. It should blow over in a couple of hours. I know a place where we can go, but you have to promise that you'll never tell anybody where it is."

She winced as the rain fell in stinging sheets against her face. Lightning flashed, sending a limb crashing just next to her feet. "If it gets me out of this rain, I promise."

He cupped her chin in his hand and lifted her eyes to meet his. "This is a solemn promise, Jillian. I need you to swear."

"Take me to this hiding place and I'll never tell a soul where it is."

Without another word, Bael slipped his arms under her knees, throwing her legs around his waist, and started running through the woods as if she weighed nothing. She yelped, curling her body around him as he moved at superhuman speed through the trees.

The rain had soaked through her clothes and though she didn't think it was possible, she was cold. The warmth of his body seeped through the sheriff's department t-shirt. She couldn't help but snuggle against him.

The farther they moved from the rift, the easier she felt. And by the time Bael skidded to a stop, chest heaving against hers, she'd almost relaxed. She lifted her head from his shoulder to see that they were in front of a large steel double door embedded in the side of a hill.

Bael set her on her feet while he approached the doors. The hill itself was weird because there was no elevation here in the bayou, only flat, marshy land. It took a few seconds of staring to realize it wasn't actually a hill. It was concrete that had been carefully obscured with live vines.

"Is this the part where you take me out to the swamp and I disappear?" she asked, looking around. She couldn't see another building or a road, just miles and miles of swamp.

"No, this is the part where we get out of the rain and you stay warm and dry. Now, please turn aside."

Jillian frowned, but turned away and heard a series of

metallic wrenching noises which she did her best to ignore in favor of dancing and rubbing her arms to keep warm.

"Okay, turn around."

She turned just in time to see Bael jerk the double doors open, revealing a dark, cavernous space. A rush of warm copper-scented air hit her in the face as he pulled her through the doors. Bael locked the door behind him and she was enclosed in this lightless void.

Panic crept up her throat. She reached for her cell phone, with its trusty flashlight feature, but she heard a loud exhalation from Bael and suddenly the space was illuminated in a golden glow. Lying before her were piles of gold as far as the eye could see, coins and platters and goblets and chests filled with jewels. She was overwhelmed by the vast size of it, shielding her eyes from the blinding reflected shine.

His face was set in an odd, nearly shy expression as he said, "This is my hoard."

She looked from the sea of gold to the flaming torch Bael was holding, back to the treasure.

"You're a dragon." She started to laugh as he stabbed the base of the torch into a pile of coins. "Of all the creatures I thought you could be, I wouldn't have guessed a dragon."

"You didn't know?" He grinned, his sharp white teeth reflecting the golden light of the torch he'd lit with his breath.

"You didn't say! No one in the Boone family has! Everybody else in town just volunteers what they are. And you have no tells and it has been so frustrating!"

Bael was doubled over with laughter, his hands braced against his knees.

"Don't you laugh at me, Bael Boone or I will take one of your coins and hide it in Zed's office somewhere."

"You wouldn't dare," he whispered, his teeth growing longer

and his voice lowering to a raspy rumble. She shivered as he leaned closer, his nose trailing along her hairline. His lips brushed along her forehead and her hands slid up his arms to pull him closer.

She lifted her head, so her breath fluttered over his lips as she said, "Keep testing me and you'll find out."

He frowned. "What else did you think I could be?"

"A lion shifter," she suggested, smirking slightly. "A tiger, a bear."

"You think I'm in the same shifter category as Zed?"

"I didn't know! You could have been anything. The golden eyes and the constant sniffing told me nothing and...so that was smoke I saw coming out of your nose." She sighed and plopped back on an enormous pile of what looked like Spanish doubloons. "Also, the dragon-themed décor around city hall makes much more sense."

And to her surprise, instead of telling her to get her ass off of his treasure, his eyes flashed that eager amber and he dropped to his knees in front of her. "Yes, those were my smoke rings. I didn't realize you saw them."

"I see a lot more than you think I do. So how does this work? We know almost nothing about dragon shifters. You're all so secretive. And when an academic tries to get too close, you've been known to turn them medium rare."

"We're just like other shifters only my form is bigger and more awesome. And I'm a little obsessive about gold or anything shiny really." He threaded his fingers through her hair, watching as the light shimmered over the shifting threads.

"How far does the cave go?"

He leaned against the coins, settling into them. "It's not so much a cave as a warehouse. Dragons are mountain creatures by nature. We can't build underground hoards here, so we make do with what we got. I tried to keep the shape irregular, so it wouldn't stand out so much against the natural backdrop. I had to dig it and pour the concrete myself, so it took a while. Dragons don't ever let anyone else know where their hoard is, you see, so I couldn't hire anyone."

"And what do you do with it?" she asked.

"I know I have it. I can provide for a mate and many children with it. That's enough."

She nodded. "That's good to know. How often do you get to come out here?"

"Not often. I don't want my cousins following me and trying to take it for their own. We have a saying, 'A worthy dragon loses not one coin.' In other words, if you're a dragon worth his wings, your hoard won't get taken from you."

"But you just like knowing it's here?" she guessed.

He nodded, his eyes flashing in the torchlight. He slid his fingers over the hem of her shirt, pulling it over her ribs, fanning his hand over them. She arched up to kiss him, his tongue sweeping into her mouth in a filthy dance. And when she ran out of air, she wrapped her arms around him to keep the warmth of his body close.

"How did you collect all of this?" She began pointing at objects she could spot in the firelight. "That scarab plaque is Egyptian. That mask is Mayan. That headdress is early Roman."

His brows rose and her shirt rose over her head. He set it aside and she was very grateful that she'd worn one of her prettier bras that day, light blue pinstripes with darker blue lace. There was a matching pair of panties, but it was laundry day so she was wearing white cotton with neon pink and green stars. Maybe she could shimmy out of them before he saw.

"Before you become a paranormal anthropologist, you have to study human history," she told him. She spread her fingers through the pile of coins they'd settled on, splashing them left and right. "And have you been raiding Spanish armadas?"

He rolled them both and leaned over her, his hands keeping

her from dropping back onto the gold. "I inherited a lot of it. I was my parents' only child. And the rest, I collected or 'requisitioned.'"

"Requisitioned?" She grinned as he leaned closer, displacing the coins with a steady *clink clink clink.*

"It's a lifetime of work," he murmured against her cheek. She leaned into him, letting his lips drag across her skin. He was warm, so warm in this cold, dark room where they were the only living things. She hissed as her bare skin came into contact with the metal. His fangs snicked into place as he hovered over her, scanning the room for the source of her distress.

"It's cold," she said, laughing and pulling his shirt over his head. His torso was just as lean and tapered as she expected, not excessively muscled, but obviously strong and possessing a certain serpentine beauty. His shoulders were tattooed with what looked like the axillaries of a pair of massive wings. She pulled him close, tracing the lines with her fingers.

He reached into the treasure pile and retrieved a bib necklace that was made of several tiers of worked gold and rough, cloudy red gemstones. It looked like something from an Etruscan etching. The light in his eyes as he fastened it around her neck bordered on obscene. She wasn't sure whether he was more entranced by her body or the sight of his gold against her skin.

Her clever fingers plucked at his jeans, popping the button loose. "Gold doesn't keep you warm. You can't eat it. It doesn't love you back. It doesn't feel."

"I don't know, it feels pretty good to me." He pushed her back. The metal slid against her skin, cushioning her, moving with her. It wasn't exactly uncomfortable, just strange, definitely unlike the soft mattresses she was used to.

"That entendre was beneath you, Sheriff."

"I've got something better beneath me," he grumbled into her skin.

She laughed. Just as he hitched her feet to balance on his thighs, the outlines of his wings grew from his back, rising as a pair of green-and-gold-scaled wings. She watched in wide-eyed wonder as those wings expanded over them, curling around them both in a protective canopy. She tried not to be distracted by the dance of color on his scales, but it was impossible. How was she supposed to concentrate on his lovely, drugging kisses when she was this close to a dragon? Or halfway to a dragon, at least.

His fingers, long and slim, slipped between thighs already dewed with anticipation. He touched her, circling the most sensitive part of her with his thumb and she gasped, throwing her head back against the gold. She rolled her hips to meet his fingertips, and the tinkling of falling coins sounded like music.

He played her, stroking and teasing, and when she finally slid his pants down his thighs, she saw why he was spending so much time preparing her. She wondered if this was typical of all dragon shifters or if Bael was just gifted. Because if women knew about dragon proportionality, the werewolf romance novel market would be completely bankrupt.

Also, she may have grabbed it in her enthusiasm.

It had been a while.

Bael gasped as her fingers wrapped around his length, gripping it tight. Her hand was slick with sweat as she let it slip through her fingers experimentally. He dragged his lips down the column of her neck, before carefully scraping his fangs over the curve of her breast. She shrieked and threw her arms around his shoulders. He thrust deep and she arched back against the coins.

His forehead was pressed against hers and he paused, giving her time to adjust. Her feet slid along his sides, locking around his hips. She took a deep breath and undulated her hips, biting her lip to keep the frantic, embarrassing sounds from escaping. Already, she could feel the pressure building inside of her in a spiraling coil of pleasure.

Now that she'd started moving, he was plunging against her in earnest. His skin was growing warmer and warmer and the outlines of the wings against his back blurred. She was sweating under his heat, their skin slipping against each other as they moved. His tongue traced the line of her jaw while his fingers threaded through her hair.

Her fingertips explored his back, caressing the smooth, glassy scales where his wings joined to his shoulders. He froze, his eyes flashing molten gold and rolling back in his head. She stroked the extension of his wings again, and he trembled, groaning into her throat.

She could feel his elongated claws scraping against her sides as his hips pistoned against her. That was going to leave a mark. Not that she cared, because every nerve in her body was firing at once, barreling toward the edge of pleasure. Tension so strong it almost hurt twisted inside of her, and expanded then contracted. She screamed, her body squeezing him tight as his movements became frantic.

Sweat cooling on her skin, she stroked her hands over his shoulders as he reared up, wings outstretched, and roared. It felt like a wildfire sweeping through her womb. She screamed in shock and he dropped over her, clutching her to him. His claws dug even deeper into her skin and she relished the tiny bit of pain to distract her from the heat inside her.

"I'm OK," she panted, running her fingers over his scalp. "I'm OK."

His wings remained curled around them as he hovered over her. Still breathing heavily, he nudged his nose against her jaw, kissing the curve of it, her cheek, her nose, her eyelids. She inhaled the smoky scent of him, gently butting her head again his chin.

Slipping out of her with a moan, he dropped down beside her, holding her to his chest. His wings slowly shrank down to a manageable size. She swallowed thickly, reaching for the backpack she'd dropped close by. She dragged out a bottle of water and drained half of it, then offered the bottle to Bael. "So your cousin Balfour is a bit of a prick isn't he?"

He snorted, spitting the water onto a nearby gold statuette of the goddess Bast. "I don't really think I want to talk about Balfour right now."

"I only thought of it because of him yelling to call when you were done with me. Even if you're done with me, please don't call him."

"I'm not done with you." Bael growled and kissed her, hard. "And I wouldn't dare."

"Thank you."

"Balfour's always been an asshole, ever since we were kids. He takes after my uncle Balthazar, who hated my father with a Biblical passion. And now, Balfour's trying to prove that I'm not dragon enough to inherit my portion of my grandfather's hoard."

"Why would he say that?" she asked.

"My mother was human. I was the only hatchling to survive their clutch. Balfour says that between my mother's dirty blood and the fact that my parents died relatively young before parenting me properly, I am cursed and will only bring bad luck to the family gold."

She scooped up a handful of coins and let them drop through her fingers. "The funny thing is that most people, when they talk about cursed treasure, they mean the treasure brings a curse on the person."

"Well, when your culture is focused on passing that gold down to your family, you worry a lot more about putting bad luck on the gold," Bael told her.

"Is inheriting your grandfather's gold important to you?"

"Yes, and not just because I'm greedy or that I want to add to my hoard. But because my father wanted me to inherit his share.

He was a good man, a better dragon. He was honorable. I would see his wishes respected," he said.

Jillian rubbed her fingers over his shoulder. "I'm sorry to hear about your family."

"I was twenty-three when they died."

"That's not considered fully parented?" she asked.

He shook his head. "Dragons have so much information to impart to their children that a dragon isn't considered fully raised until he's at least thirty. It's not unreasonable, considering our long life spans."

"How long do you live?" she asked.

"Not important."

Jillian's voice rose slightly. "How old are you now?"

"Eighty or so."

Her jaw dropped open. "I feel like I'm robbing the grave."

He smacked her bared ass cheek, making her yelp and then giggle.

"That thing you said earlier about human females only being able to carry one egg at a time, what was that about?" she asked.

Bael shifted uncomfortably, averting his gaze.

"I wouldn't have to ask if you dragons would share a little academic information now and then," she told him.

He rubbed a hand over her stomach, cradling it around her hip. "A female dragon only lays eggs once or twice a lifetime, which is okay because she can lay three or four eggs at a time. Male dragons that mate with human females have very low birth rates. The females cannot carry more than one hatchling at a time, and the live births tend to produce babies that have dragon traits, but who can't shift."

"What about female dragons who mate with human males?"

"They have even lower birthrates but a higher rate of shifters. The theory is that it's time in the egg, warm in the nest while the mother dragon is sitting on it, that transfers the magic. And I'm sure, after the little scene in the coffee shop today, Balfour's gonna claim that I'm taking a human mate, dishonoring my family even more."

"Is that just the regular interspecies racism or a desire to preserve the species?"

"A little bit of both. With the birth rates dropping, I'm expected to marry a nice dragon girl from another town, so my children can shift."

"Well, that's a shame. No dragon babies for me, I guess," she snorted.

And while she'd meant it as a flippant joke, he gave her a tender smile. "No, there's a few more steps to it, if I wanted to get you pregnant."

"What sort of steps?" she gasped. "Would it involve telling me your true dragon name?"

He laughed, but given the way he balked at the mention of his true name, Jillian thought maybe she'd touched on something true.

"I'm not going to tell you everything!"

"Oh come on, it's for science!" she cried.

"I don't think there's any way that information will fit into your report to the League," he told her.

"You never know! I might do a whole chapter on mating rituals. I'm wily and unpredictable," she said, giving him an arch look.

He laughed and kissed her cheeks, but she pressed on. "I will not be distracted, Sheriff!"

But he just kept kissing her and she definitely ended up distracted. She noticed that the longer Bael laid on the pile of coins, the warmer it got, to the point that it was almost comfortable. She burrowed against his chest and wondered if she could actually sleep like this.

"So how did you get into studying *magie* creatures?" he asked, playing with a lock of her hair.

"Meaning, how did a nice girl like me end up in a field like this?"

"That's what I'm asking. I know almost nothing about you, except for what your League bio says. I don't know where you're from or anything about your family or any of the things people usually know about each other before they..."

"Have sex on a big pile of treasure, Scrooge McDuck-style?"

As he goggled at her, she laughed and tucked her head under his chin. "I've mentioned I'm from Ohio."

"That tells me nothing."

"I'm from Loveland, Ohio. Ever since the fifties, people have said that they've seen a creature that looks like a four-foot tall frog, walking around on its hind legs. There've been several sightings over the years, but it's usually near a bridge on the little Miami River. I'd been hearing the stories since I was a kid. People used to dare each other to go walk on 'the bridge' where the frog man supposedly lived. The problem being that there's lots of bridges on the Little Miami River. And being the detail-oriented person that I was, it really bugged me that none of stories matched up—the locations were always different, the descriptions of the frog man, whether he looked more like a lizard or a frog. So I started looking at all the bridges on the little Miami River. I spent afternoons after school, riding my bike around looking for clues, picking holes in the stories that my friends told me."

He nodded. "Yeah, that sounds like you."

She smacked his chest. "And then one evening, I lingered just a little too long by this one particular bridge, because I found a weird stash of fishing equipment hidden by one of the supports. Throw nets and a sort of trident made out of bamboo. Everybody I knew who fished did it with cane poles and crickets. I'd never even seen a trident in real life. So, I'm documenting this stuff, taking pictures and sketches. And while I'm distracted, it got really dark. And of course, when I tried to go home, my bike tire was flat. And because I was very poorly supervised, I couldn't get a hold of my parents. I'm just sitting there, on the side of the road with no way to get home and somebody else's fishing equipment around my feet. I'm distracted on my phone, trying to find somebody to come pick me up. That's when I hear someone trying to move that trident, dragging the bamboo across the asphalt. I turned around and saw this short little bald man with huge hands. He had these weirdly long fingers wrapped around the trident and looked like he was about to swing it at me. I promptly passed out and whacked my head on a rock."

"I woke up and I met Mel Yamagita, who was an orthopedist living in Loveland. He felt bad about scaring me and he didn't feel right about leaving me unconscious on the side of the road in the dark. So he built a little fire, did some fishing and waited for me to wake-up. He was a kappa, one of the Japanese water creatures? His family had lived in Loveland for the better part of fifty years, and they liked to spend their spare time on the river, fishing in their natural forms. And you can't do that without getting spotted a few times. Hence, the frog man legend."

"You found the Loveland Frog, when you were a teenager?"

"I asked him a bunch of a questions, where he was from, how his transformation worked, why he hid the fishing equipment instead of taking it with him. And he answered all of them. Of course, the known mythology only got half of the information about kappas right. I think he was relieved to finally have someone to talk to about it. I think he was lonely. His family had died over the years and he didn't know any other shifters or creatures in the area. I asked him why he was telling me all of this and he said, 'Who's going to believe you?' And he was right, no one would. I started meeting Mel for fishing every few weeks. He'd tell me about all of the other creatures that were real. Shifters and witches and dragons. It was fascinating. I majored in folklore, got my PhD from George Washington University. And if you knew who to ask and where to apply, you could get recruited for internships at the League. I did well there, and here we are."

He stroked her hair back from her face. "So you were destined for this life."

"I honestly think I was. I know you don't think much of the League, but I found a community with them. I found a place where I wasn't the weird girl obsessed with folk tales and monsters. I found my best friend, Sonja. My work and my interests weren't something I had to hide. They were celebrated."

"I don't care for the League because I don't like the idea that people we had no part in choosing appointed themselves the authority over us."

"I can understand that."

"So what did you mean earlier, about you being so poorly supervised as a minor that you had time to go searching bridges for monsters?" he asked.

Jillian's expression turned pensive. "My family wasn't exactly the kind of people that you have here in Mystic Bayou. I mean, we had a nice house in a fancy neighborhood, but it was always empty. It wasn't that my parents were cruel, but they made it clear that they'd rather be somewhere else. My dad was always at work. My mom was too busy with whatever charitable project she was working on to be home. I was alone most of time, and neither of them noticed. They were lucky that I channeled my loneliness into studying and not drugs or some other self-destructive extracurricular activity. By the time I got through my undergrad, I just stopped inviting them to graduation and ceremonies because I was tired of them not showing up. I think it made them happy that they didn't have to make excuses anymore. We haven't spoken in six years. No particularly angry words when we parted. We just stop pretending to make the effort."

"Sometimes apathy hurts just as much as cruelty. At least when someone is yelling, you can imagine that they care."

She nodded. "What about your family?"

"Complicated. There are generations and branches and inner circles. And they're all competing for money, attention and honor. There's no love there, just a gravity that seems to hold everybody together."

"I think that's the way it is in most families, to different degrees."

"Zed's family isn't like that," Bael muttered.

"Then Zed's a lucky guy. Should we go back now?" she asked. "It sounds like the rain has stopped."

Bael looked vaguely offended by the suggestion. "If you'd like."

"I think I would," she said, smiling as she threaded her fingers through his. "I've got a lot of data I need to analyze."

"But no dragon sex chapter," he told her sternly.

She sighed dramatically. "Fine, tie my hands."

He kissed her again. "Later, if you want."

10

BAEL

Bael parked outside of the iron gates of his grandfather's estate, River Rest, preparing himself for a less than pleasant evening. It was one of the more opulent homes in the parish, a two-story pristine white mansion built in the grand antebellum style, located at the mouth of the Fool's Blood River. The only concession to the family's heritage was the golden dragon perched on the non-traditional dome at the top of the house.

Breathing deeply, Bael rolled a smooth golden ball inset with opals in his hand. It had once been a toy to some pampered Germanic princess, but he'd turned it into the dragon version of a stress ball. This dinner with his grandfather couldn't have come at a worse possible time. He'd been increasingly tense for days, and as much as he hated to admit it, it was all centered on the little blond scientist.

He hadn't seen Jillian in the days since their tryst in his cave. She'd been holed up at Miss Lottie's house, working, or traveling all over the parish conducting her interviews. She'd taken his calls. She'd been her own sweet-and-sour self, teasing him and laughing at his jokes. But when he'd suggested that she come to his house for dinner or join him at the pie shop for lunch, she'd put him off—politely, but, firmly—in favor of her work.

Bael didn't understand this response. She'd laid with him in his gold. He'd let her see that part of his life, trusted her with the location of his treasure. They shared what he considered to be a beautiful moment, and then she got up, put her clothes on and asked him to take her home, like they'd spent the rainy afternoon playing *Monopoly*.

How was it that she'd spent her lifetime studying the *magique*, and yet, she didn't seem to understand what a gesture he had made, taking her to his hoard? He was offering to share his life with her, his treasure. There was no greater offering his kind could make, and he was making it even after explaining the reservations that dragons had against human mates.

She'd wanted him. She'd responded so enthusiastically, so sweetly, and she wasn't cruel enough to fake that. Right? Had he offended her, taking her so roughly in his cave? Maybe his treasure wasn't impressive enough for her: she didn't seem like the type of woman who wanted to depend on a man, but maybe she required more? Would she go to some other dragon, seeking a greater hoard? Maybe Balfour? After all, she was the one who brought his cousin up with Bael's sweat still drying on her skin.

He felt a dull pain in his palm and realized he'd crushed the gold ball he was holding. Then he grimaced and stashed it in his glovebox.

No, Jillian wasn't a "dragon rider," Balfour's clever little derogatory term for human women who wanted a fling with a dragon. She simply didn't understand his offer. Dragons were a secretive lot. They didn't share their private lives with their neighbors. They didn't shift in front of non-dragons, unless they were mated into the family. They didn't share their festivals. They didn't discuss their courting rituals, unless those mating rituals were being offered to a non-dragon.

He supposed he couldn't get too upset with her for not understanding. He just had to make her understand. He would appeal to her with facts and science, and possibly a pie chart and graphs. She loved pie charts and graphs.

As much as he shrugged off Zed's teasing on the subject, Bael could admit to himself that he was more than a little bit in love with her. He thought maybe he'd loved her since the minute he'd seen her telling Zed off in City Hall. He loved her fire and her brains and that damnable curiosity that always seemed to annoy him in the moment, but fascinated him in the long-term. As long as it didn't affect him directly. She was beautiful, yes, but the treasure he sought was inside of her.

She would probably punch him if she heard him saying that.

Though the desire to turn his truck around and drive to *le maison de fous* to talk to her was very strong, he punched the eight-digit code (yes, *eight* digits) on his grandfather's gate and started up the winding driveway. He was a desperate dragon, but he still had a little bit of pride.

That pride almost deflated when he saw several cars belonging to his aunts, uncles and cousins. He should have known Baldric Boone wouldn't allow a solo visit when he wanted a full family gathering. The fact that Bael might not have the patience or desire to see the entire Boone clan *en masse* wouldn't occur to the dragon patriarch. It wasn't that he didn't love his family...in select groups...in small doses... on federally recognized holidays.

Bael had been putting this off for weeks. In fact, he'd pulled out of the family meeting Balfour had tried to summon him to, claiming he was too busy with work. That was another concept that was outside his family's grasp. The Boones owned their own businesses. They did not have bosses. When they wanted time off, they simply closed up shop.

If his parents were still alive, he wouldn't mind visiting so much. Yes, the evening would have still been marked by the usual passive-aggressive sniping and under-handed power plays, but he would have had the amusement of watching his father ignore the jibes entirely while uncle Benedict seethed. He would have had the pleasure of watching his mother spar with his aunts, insulting them without their realizing it. He would have had them to talk it over and laugh with afterwards, while eating his mother's home-made ice cream.

His mother, Erin, had been a rare gem, beautiful and kind and funny. His father had credited her influence for giving Bael a more sympathetic nature than the average Boone, for thinking of other people before thinking of himself. Erin's father had held the office of sheriff a few decades before Bael had been elected.

He wondered how Jillian would fare if he brought her into the dragon pit. He hated the idea of subjecting her to his aunts' sneers, but at the same time, he could very easily see her blithely ignoring them. And then insisting that they all fill out a questionnaire.

The family was encamped on the stone chaises his late grandmother had installed on the west lawn, near the river, around a fire pit. A whole ox, no doubt provided by their uncle Barnabas's butcher shop, cooked over the fire pit, perfuming the air with the homey smell of roasting meat. They were surrounded by a circle of iron torches meant to lend a cheerful light to the proceedings, but they only cast sinister looking shadows over his family's angular faces.

His grandfather, Baldric, a tall, lean man with a headful of silver hair, rose from the central chaise, crossing the lawn with a confident stride that belied his nearly two hundred years of life. His grandfather's eyes flashed red in the firelight, but he hugged his grandson tight, bumping foreheads with him. Over Baldric's shoulder, Bael could see his cousin glaring at them.

"I see the whole family came to join us," Bael noted. "Despite the fact that you told me it would just be us."

Grandfather Baldric shrugged. "Your aunt Bathtilda asked what my plans were for the evening and when she heard you would be here, she wanted to organize a better dinner than an old widower like me could provide."

"It would really be nice to have a conversation with you that wasn't overheard by about a dozen eavesdroppers, *Farfar*," Bael said.

"What can you say to me that you can't say in front of the clan?" Baldric asked, his eyes twinkling as they walked at a snail's pace toward the circle.

"Lots of things. *Lots* of them."

Baldric huffed, "Could it be something about that *drole* girl you've been spending time with? Balfour says you've been seeing a lot of her lately."

Bael's mind flashed to exactly how much of Jillian he'd seen, which was not an appropriate subject to think on in front of his grandfather. Bael silently gave thanks that his kind wasn't telephathic like some of the species in Mystic Bayou. He didn't want anyone in his family to see that much of Jillian, either.

"Balfour needs to mind his own business."

"Can't see why someone your age would want to waste his time with someone he can't breed with," Baldric said. "You're in the prime of your life. She's human. She's not fit to carry your young. No grandson of mine is going to inherit my hoard if he mates with a human."

Every muscle in Bael's face was rigid as he said, "My mother was human."

"And look how that turned out. One living hatchling before she died. And then your father couldn't go on without her. Because he *loved* her too much. Nothing but disaster and ruin from that pairing."

Out of deference for his grandfather's age, Bael did not growl or bare his teeth. This was the darker side of his clan, the part that gave him relief when his family declined to fully assimilate in the community. If they fully engaged with their neighbors, the locals would realize exactly how much contempt the Boones had for anyone that wasn't them.

"As the result of their pairing, I would disagree," Bael told him.

"Oh, don't take it personally, boy. You know what I thought of your mama. She was a fine woman, for a human, just not what I would have chosen for my son. You're lucky that you can shift as easily as you do. You could have gone your whole life without knowing that joy."

"Because my mother was a lot stronger than you gave her credit for." Bael's tone was firm and left no room for argument.

Baldric waved his hand dismissively. "A happy coincidence. I want you to choose better than your father. Make a match with one of the New Country clans. You know that they've made inquiries about you and Balfour over the years. Your cousin has agreed to review their offers."

"I'll bet," Bael muttered.

"You should let me arrange a match for you as well."

Bael frowned.

"At least consider it," Baldric said, nudging at him.

Bael opened his mouth to answer but his cell phone rang in his pocket. He pulled it out and noted Zed's name on the caller ID.

"Is it a mark of a respectful grandson to let a phone call interrupt an important conversation with his *farfar*?" Baldric sniffed.

"It's Zed. He knows I'm with you tonight and he would only call if it was important parish business."

"Important parish business. No such thing."

"It will only take a minute," Bael said, walking briskly away from his family and answering the phone. "Please tell me there is some legitimate reason for me to come running to you for reasons of vital public service."

To his surprise, Zed didn't even chuckle. "It's Gladys Fider. You need to come to her house, right now."

A SHORT TIME LATER, Bael whipped his truck into Gladys's gravel driveway. He hadn't bothered with lights and sirens. Zed had made it clear that it was too late to help Miss Gladys.

Bael's family had been just as understanding about his departure as he'd expected, which was not at all. He couldn't exactly tell them what was going on, because he didn't know. And as far as they were concerned, nothing happening within the community of Mystic Bayou could be as important as socializing with *them*. He was bone tired already and he knew his difficult night had just begun.

Zed was sitting on the front porch, his face in his hands. The porch light cast a silver corona over his dark hair. When Bael approached, Zed lifted his head and there were tears in his eyes. Bael rocked back on his heels. He'd known the bear shifter for more than thirty years and he'd never seen him cry before.

"You all right?"

"Not really. I've known Miss Gladys since I was a cub. She wouldn't hurt a fly. She taught arts and crafts classes at the elementary school, for gods' sake. Why would anyone want to do this to her? What kind of town are we living in now, Bael?"

"I don't know," Bael said, putting his hand on his shoulder. "How'd you get the call?"

"There was no call. My *maman* sent me over here because Gladys needed some new curtains hung up. She didn't answer the door and I went around back and saw her through the porch door."

"Can you show me?"

Zed sighed and sniffed, but then nodded and led Bael around to the back porch. The door was standing open. The lights were on and the television was set on the Oprah network. A widow, Miss Gladys had been serving herself a solitary dinner of fried shrimp when she'd been attacked. The plate was still sitting on the counter, still waiting for a squeeze of lemon.

Gladys had been left stretched out on her kitchen table, still dressed in her housecoat. A long incision split her torso. Unlike Ted, there were no frenzied cuts on Gladys. She was still recognizable. Her blood had dripped over the table and onto the floor, but Bael noted that there were no footprints on the linoleum. There was a large squarish smear on the floor, as if someone had put a piece of plastic or cardboard near the table before cutting her open. Bael snapped on a pair of latex gloves and handed Zed the camera.

"The door was standing open," Zed noted.

Bael nodded. "Nobody forced their way in. Nothing is tossed around. There's no defensive wounds, so she didn't fight."

Zed gulped. "So does that mean that she knew whoever did this? One of our own?"

"Could be. It also could just be that she was a nice, trusting old woman who believed she was safe in her own kitchen. Some people around here still don't lock their doors, Zed."

"We may have to do something about that," Zed sighed. "We were able to write Ted off as a fluke, but I don't think it would be responsible if these attacks continue. As much as I hate it, people around here need to be more cautious if we have a killer running around. Should we hold a town meeting? Put a notice in the newspaper? Establish a curfew? I don't want to be the mayor from *Jaws*, Bael."

"I don't know. All that and more, maybe. For right now, let's just record the evidence we have. And then we'll call David Wyatt to collect her body."

They worked a grid around the kitchen, from the door to the table, photographing and collecting everything out of place. Bael avoided looking at the body for as long as possible before he finally had to record her position and assess the gore. How many more of these attacks would there be? Why had the killer chosen Ted and Gladys? They were different races, genders and shifter specification. Hell, they voted for different parties. They had nothing in common, other than they were both over the age of fifty. He tried to wrack his brain for some little detail that could lead to this situation making sense, but he was coming up dry.

"Look at this," Zed said, pointing under the table and looking green beneath his beard. There was a crumpled sheet of paper just outside of the pool of dried blood. He carefully plucked the paper from under the table and unfolded it. The page was covered in nonsensical symbols and random letters.

He had Zed photograph the page and then slid it into an evidence bag.

"It looks like a page from one of those little notebooks Jillian uses to take notes." Bael's head snapped up, the color draining from his face. "Jillian."

"I already called Jillian, she's fine. My *maman* went to pick her up and took her to spend the night at her cave. She'll be the safest girl in the parish."

"Thanks, man."

"Hey, you finally found a girl that makes you worry and go all gooey and stupid. I'm not giving that up. It's comedy gold."

Bael laughed, relieved to feel some emotion other than horror. "You're an asshole."

"So how are things going there?" Zed asked.

Bael gestured toward Gladys's prone form. "This conversation seems inappropriate."

"Come on, man. I know it's not super sensitive, but I need something else to focus on. Anything else. Did you really show her your treasure? I've been begging to see your hoard and you always said no. But with more cuss words."

Bael's face flushed an angry magenta. He'd trusted Jillian with the greatest of secrets and she shared that with Zed of all people? "Did she tell you that?"

Zed grinned at him. "No, but you just did."

Bael hissed out a curse. "You suck."

"She didn't tell me anything. But I just sensed a sort of... Well, lately, you've been smiling like guy who just got laid. And since you're someone who doesn't display much in the way of emotions, I find that amusing. Is she gonna stay in town after her report's done?"

Bael shook his head and went back to his evidence. "Yeah, I'm not talking about this."

"Well, I wouldn't mind if she stayed in town and laid your eggs. She's funny and sweet. And you turn such awesome colors when we talk about her."

"We're no longer friends."

11

JILLIAN

Jillian sipped some Mylanta straight from the bottle and adjusted her van seat back from the steering wheel. She wasn't sure there was enough room for her stomach.

She'd been staying at the mama bear's house for the past three days and had been fed until she thought she'd pass out. Clarissa apparently believed that if you didn't have to roll a guest out of your house like the blueberry girl in *Willy Wonka,* you were a bad hostess. Frankly, Jillian had felt a little kidnapped after Clarissa strode into her house, told her to pack up all her "science-y things" while Clarissa rifled through her drawers and packed her a bag. While Jillian stood protesting, with her laptop clutched to her chest like a baby, Clarissa tucked Jillian under the arm not occupied by her duffel and carried Jillian out like a naughty cub.

Clarissa wouldn't explain why she was abducting Jillian, leaving that to Zed when he dropped by the house later to tell her about poor Miss Gladys. She'd met Gladys at the pie shop earlier week to discuss her "new lifestyle," being able to turn into a bipedal porcupine whenever she was angry. Like the Hulk, but sharper. She'd seemed like a perfectly nice old widow, though she'd mentioned a few times that she hoped there might be a cure someday for "remade *magique*."

Knowing that the town hadn't had a murder in years, only to have two people, both of whom she'd had contact with, both killed in a particularly vicious fashion, filled her with a peculiar guilt and dread. What if this was her fault? What if she'd stirred some ugly old grudge within the community that led to the deaths of two nice elderly people?

Zed assured her that this wasn't the case, that what she was doing was important and that the town needed the assistance the League would provide.

"Ted and Gladys gave you their stories because they believed in what you're doing, because they liked you and thought you would do them justice. They believed that the town needed the help the League was going to give us. If you give up now, that's the only way you could disappoint them. Now, did Gladys or Ted have anything strange to say when you interviewed them? Did they feel like someone was watching them or following them? Did they mention feeling unsafe?"

Jillian shook her head. "No, Gladys was a little reserved. I think she wasn't thrilled about being able to change forms but she accepted it. She never asked 'why me?' She mentioned hoping to find a cure one day. I only spoke to Ted briefly at the dance, but he seemed really happy as a *magie*. He said it was like being a teenager all over again." She sniffed lightly, her eyes shining with unshed tears. "They were just a couple of sweet people who didn't seem to want to hurt anybody. And I can't seem to sit down and write about them without crying. I can't tell Bael because he already seems so stressed out. And I know it's wrong to dump this all on you, but if I tell your mom, she's just going to try to feed me more."

"Aw, *catin*." Zed held her to his chest, even as it shook with laughter, and stroked her hair. "I'm sorry. You're holding up just fine. You're gonna be okay and you're gonna do a fine job. Don't you doubt it. And try to share these things with Bael, no matter how stressed he seems. I don't think he'd like it much if you poured your heart out to me, instead of him."

"You're probably right."

She'd been mollified by his earnestness and the hugs, but she had to admit that she'd gone to bed that night on a pile of furs Clarissa kept in the guest-cave, and cried her eyes out. And then Clarissa woke her up and Jillian ate her feelings. For three days.

Hence her heartburn.

Having finally convinced the Berends that it was safe for her to go to her rental house, she'd come to town to sit in on the public information meeting Zed and Bael had arranged to discuss the "situation" with the locals. Bael and Zed were trying to prevent a panic, and she admired that. But she found that she just couldn't walk into the pie shop to listen to Bael assure his neighbors that everything was fine, when she knew it was not.

So here she sat, in her van, trying to determine whether to drive home or pop into the Boone Mercantile and Grocery for more Mylanta. She heard her name being called through the cracked window and turned to see Bonita De Los Santos waving at her from the front of the post office.

She rolled down her window to hear her call, "Miss Jillian, I've got something for you! Actually, I've got two somethings for you. All the way from Washington, D.C.!"

A large woman with a perpetual crown of braided salt-and-pepper hair, Bonita was a touch-know psychic who kept informed of all the news in town simply by touching the envelopes as she sorted. She knew who owed money, who was getting love notes from people they weren't married to, and whose kids were getting into college. But she took the confidentiality of her job very seriously, she'd told Jillian during her interview. She never told a soul what she learned from the mail, even if they offered her cash or *boudin.*

"How are you holdin' up, honey?" Bonita asked.

Jillian smiled wearily. "I'm all right, Miss Bonita. How are you?"

"Oh, everybody who's come in today has been talking about poor Ted and Gladys. It's a heartbreaking thing, to have two of our own taken from us. But the town's been through worse than this. Hurricanes, plagues, the War of Northern Aggression. We'll lock our doors, keep a watch over the people we love and we'll get through it, just like everything else."

Jillian nodded, her shoulders feeling a little lighter as she crossed the street and entered the tiny post office, which Jillian suspected was original to the early settlement days of *le Lieu Mystique.* Under the space where most post offices hung wanted posters, Bonita had written "Mind Your Business and Move Along" in bold Sharpie print.

"I'm not really expecting anything from my office, Miss Bonita."

Bonita heaved a toaster-oven-sized box onto her counter. It was stamped with "Handle with Care!" and "This Side Up!" and "Perishable! Keep in Cool Dry Place!"

"Oh, honey, it's not from your office. It's personal. Both of them are. I just thought I'd save myself the drive all the way out to Miss Lottie's place," Bonita told her.

The other box was much more subtly appointed and labeled with Sonja's impossibly neat handwriting. Both boxes had been shipped "express high-priority speed," whatever that meant.

Jillian's eye narrowed. "How much did you see?"

Bonita's expression was sympathetic. "Enough to know that you're not gonna be happy when you open one of them."

"Should I have you open it?"

"No, that's not my business. I just wanted to forewarn you. I find it helps people not to feel so sucker-punched," Bonita told her.

Jillian took the rather elegant pearl-handled letter opener Bonita was offering and cut the box tape open. The return address read "Swirls and Sprinkles" in Crystal City. The box contained a dozen carefully packaged cupcakes from her favorite bakery from home, plus multiple dry ice packs to keep the buttercream frosting from melting.

She pulled a note from the desk of Tate Ashford, Esq., out of the box. *Hey Sweet Cheeks.* Jillian groaned. She'd always hated that freaking nickname. "*I called Sonja because I couldn't get you on your cell.*"

"Of course you called, because your evil ex-boyfriend super powers helped you sense that I was attracted to another man and you had to put a stop to it," she muttered.

She says you're in the middle of nowhere and I shouldn't call you, because you don't have any reception.

"More like Sonja told you not to call me because she would gladly set you on fire with the power of her brain."

But I thought that you would appreciate a little taste of home. I know what a sweet tooth you have and how mad you got when I ate your chocolate cupcake that time. It's those little things about you that I miss, the little quirks that drive me nuts when we're together, but I miss when you're not with me. I think I made a mistake, breaking things off with you, and I think I should come visit you and talk about-

She slammed the note down on the counter. "Nope." She shook her head. "Nope."

Of course Tate would claim that he broke up with her, instead of the other way around. Of course Tate thought he'd "made a mistake" breaking up with her. He frequently came to this epiphany if he thought she was dating someone else or she might forget about him. And the cute little story about how mad she'd gotten about him eating her cupcake? It had been her birthday cupcake that Sonja had left on the counter as a surprise for her. She'd come into the kitchen, dressed for a date with Tate to find him eating it. Somehow, he managed to turn her irritation over his selfishness into a charming little anecdote about how irascible she was.

"I'm sorry, honey," Bonita said, patting Jillian's hand. "I did warn you."

She nodded. "You did. Did your visions happen to show you how utterly lacking in self-awareness and ability to boyfriend this person is?"

Bonita pursed her lips. "I'm not sure that I know what that means."

Jillian pasted on a smile. "It's okay. Miss Bonita, would you like a dozen cupcakes? They're from one of my favorite bakeries back home. But for reasons I'm sure you can see, I don't think I can stomach them."

"Oh, that's so sweet of you! I could take them over to my grandkids and they would be pleased as punch."

"Tell the kids I hope they enjoy them. Tell their mother I'm sorry about the sugar high."

"Eh, my daughter-in-law has it coming. She doesn't think I know what she's been up to on the internet."

"Wow." Jillian laughed as she grabbed Sonja's package and backed out of the post-office. "Mothers-in-law in Mystic Bayou take it to a whole new level."

Bonita cackled. "Yes, we do!"

"I am better off single," Jillian sighed, pulling her phone out of her bag while she kept her package under her arm. She had a whopping two bars of reception and rejoiced, calling Sonja's number.

Sonja's smoky voice rolled into her ear. "Sweetie! I've missed you! How are your beautiful, built bayou beaus?"

Jillian unlocked the van and dropped the care package in the passenger seat. Closing the door, she smiled sweetly at Enola Pelz, one of the bear-shifter matrons she'd met at Clarissa's crawfish boil. Enola smiled and waved back, slowing down ever so slightly as Jillian asked, "I'm fine and I love you, but don't distract me with your brilliant alliterations. Why is my ex-boyfriend sending me some sort of misguided baked love offering?"

The other end of the line was silent for such a long time, Jillian had time to get into the van, where her conversation wouldn't be overheard by Enola's super naturally gifted ears. "He did what?"

"He sent me a box of cupcakes from Swirls and Sprinkles, with the kind of packaging that makes the rush shipping cost like an extra fifty bucks. How did he even find me? Did you tell him where I am?"

"No, you know I wouldn't do that... Aw, that sonofabitch. He came to the apartment the other day and I was sending you a care package. I was labeling the box when he knocked on the door. I didn't even think about him seeing it. I just can't even believe he would send you cupcakes, after that shit he pulled on your birthday."

"Right?!" Jillian cried. "Thank you. Like it's some sweet little relationship story and not another example of why *I* broke up with *him*."

"He's still claiming he broke things off?" Sonja sighed. "I'm sorry, hon. He's a useless, spineless, brainless prick, doing what useless, spineless, brainless pricks do."

Jillian sighed. This was the basis of her friendship with Sonja, something Tate never got, the neurological accord between their two brains. Sonja understood how Jillian thought and why she thought it, and even if Sonja didn't agree with Jillian's thoughts, she validated them. "Thank you."

"Did you open your present yet?"

"Crap, I'm sorry, I was so pissed off at Tate, I just—"

"No, this is better, I can hear your reactions. You're using your Swiss Army Knife keychain to cut through the tape, aren't you?"

Jillian pulled her trusty pocket-knife away from the box. "No."

"Yes you are, and I love it, because I've missed your predictable preparedness, which has been sorely lacking around the office lately. Come on, woman, just open it."

As soon as the tape gave way, Jillian cried, "Oh, you didn't!"

Jillian pulled a plushy version of Drogon, the black and red dragon from *Game of Thrones,* from the box and cuddled him to her chest. "I love him!"

"I got him from that online geek emporium you like so much. I figured if we can't binge-watch G.o.T. together, you can at least snuggle up and put your cold feet on someone who won't complain about it."

"I have a circulatory condition," Jillian shot back as she dug into the box. Sonja had sent her favorite brand of lavender Earl Grey tea, novelty socks with obscene phrases on them, some honey-based lip balm from a hippie herbalist shop they loved in Georgetown, and her mother's secret recipe spice cookies.

"You have feet colder than the Wall, woman."

"You shipped me *pryaniki,* so I forgive your harsh foot hate," Jillian sighed, prying open the Tupperware container and shoving one into her mouth. Her voice was muffled by cookie when she added, "I love you. You are my favorite person. This is a far superior baked love offering, compared to Tate's."

When Jillian opened her eyes, she realized that Enola was still standing there on the sidewalk, watching Jillian cuddle a stuffed animal to her chest while moaning over cookies. Jillian waggled her fingers. Enola grinned and walked away.

"Oh, and Mel didn't realize you'd already left for your assignment and sent you something he'd knitted. I told him I would send it along to you."

Jillian lifted what looked like a cozy for her earbuds made from multicolored eyelash yarn. "This is your fault for suggesting he take that class at the senior center."

"He's retired! He needs something to keep those long froggy fingers flexible."

"Okay, Sonja, you only alliterate this much when you're nervous, what's up?"

"Are you somewhere you won't be overheard?" Sonja asked, lowering her voice.

"I am now, yes."

Sonja whispered, "I want you to look in the bottom of the box, inside the manila envelope marked 'MONTHLY BILLS.'"

"What's going on?" Jillian tore open the envelope and found several printed interoffice emails from the League administrators. Sonja had thoughtfully highlighted the portions that mentioned Jillian by name. This was what happened when you roomed with the child of a Cold War-era spy. A care package was never just a care package.

"Your name is being whispered in the halls and it's not a good thing. The Powers That Be are not happy with the fact that you're involved in a murder investigation and that one of your subjects has turned up dead. I just transcribed a memo where two board members suggested replacing you with another anthropologist."

Jillian gasped, deeply offended. "But I didn't hurt anybody!"

"I know that. But the board wants results and they want them now. Akako Tomita herself asked to review your proposal for the Chile expedition."

Akako Tomita was the head of the League's DC board. She was an intimidating, beautiful *kitsune*, who sounded oddly like Helen Mirren, despite the fact she had the physical appearance of a twenty-five-year-old Japanese woman. Jillian had never spoken to her directly because Jillian was a junior researcher and junior researchers didn't have the clearance to talk to Akako Tomita.

Jillian feebly protested, "I've only been here a few weeks."

"They're going to call you Thursday and request a preliminary report about the population, species represented and basic cooperative systems. Use all of the discussed bullet points I highlighted in the emails. I made you a list, which I included in the envelope. You need to have it ready to go the minute they ask for it. Any delay will give them the excuse they need to recall you."

Jillian pinched the bridge of her nose and leaned back in the seat. "Maybe they should recall me."

"Don't talk like that. You're doing a great job. You said yourself that the information you're gathering is amazing."

"I'm way over my head here, Sonja. People are dying and even to the casual observer, it seems to be connected to the work I'm doing. Maybe if someone else was here, it would stop."

"And maybe pieces of a satellite will crash into someone's house tomorrow and you could make that your fault, too."

"Again, harsh," Jillian said dryly.

"I'm just saying that unless you're putting a sign on people's houses that says, 'Hey, come murder this person who talked to me,' it's not your fault. You know I love you and don't like to criticize you when you're going through one of your inevitable existential crises, but it's just a little self-indulgent to make a murder spree about you."

Jillian pressed her lips together in a thin line and inhaled deeply through her nose. "OK, you may have a point."

"Stop taking the weight of the world on your shoulders. Let murderers take accountability for their own actions."

Jillian sighed. "Why are our conversations never normal?"

"Normal doesn't exist. It was a rumor started by McCarthy in the 1950s."

"Spoken like an employee of an international shadow agency." Jillian started the van. "Thank you for saving my job."

"Any time. Go snuggle your dragon."

"Yeah, it's funny you say that..."

Sonja, whose gossip senses were highly attuned, gasped. "What?"

"I figured out what kind of shifter Bael is, or at least, he showed me."

"Ohhhh." Sonja purred. "And what did he show you?"

"He's a dragon shifter," she said. "His whole family, dragons, with the wings and everything."

"Really? But they're so secretive!"

"Well, it took him a really long time to tell me."

"So how is that going?"

"There have been some interesting developments."

"You totally let that dragon guy into your treasure box, didn't you?"

Jillian squealed. "He used his wings in weird ways and I liked it. KThanksBye!"

"What? Wings? Details! Don't you dare hang up!"

Jillian guffawed as she pressed "end."

She sighed. "I really needed that."

LATER, Jillian was sitting at her kitchen table in her panties and an OSU t-shirt, because somehow, it had gotten even hotter and more humid over the course of the day. She'd gone home directly after Sonja's call to start working on her progress report. She'd already completed two of Sonja's bullet points, species represented and government services integration. She would complete religious interaction before the end of the night, and then finish the rest of the report by the next night.

"I will not be out-brain-maneuvered," she muttered as she typed just a little harder than was strictly necessary. "This progress report will make Akako Tomita herself weep with gratitude that the League hired me. Okay, probably not because Akako Tomita is a scary badass who makes business suits look like armor... And I'm talking to myself, which is not something that amazing anthropological geniuses do."

She stood to retrieve some iced tea from her ancient fridge, but stopped when she heard footsteps on her porch steps. Why hadn't she heard a car pull up? She reached for the large butcher knife in her knife drawer and pulled it out. She crept closer to her front door, swallowing around the thick lump in her throat, wishing for once that she had a window in the door. Her legs shook under the weight of the icy fear sinking through her middle.

"Jillian?"

Her head dropped to her chest. She knew that voice. She yanked the front door open to reveal Bael walking up to her door.

"Are you *insane*?" she yelped.

Bael didn't even pause at the doorway, just picked her up by the waist and threw her legs around his hips. He crushed her mouth to his, while walking toward the stairs. She gasped and he took the opportunity to sweep his tongue into her mouth in a devastating lash. He must have removed his gun-belt in the car because she didn't feel it digging into her as he moved. There was a level of presumption there she was willing to forgive if he kept doing that thing with his tongue.

Also, point of fact, she wasn't wearing anything but panties and a t-shirt, which made his job of undressing her too easy, even while carrying her upstairs. She moved to wrap her arm around his neck and realized she was still holding the butcher knife. Naked with a butcher knife and a dragon. Was this real life?

She dropped the knife over the bannister and hoped she remembered to pick it up in the morning. The back of her head thwacked against the bedroom door as his hand scrabbled for the knob.

She yanked at his belt buckle and shimmied his pants down enough to let his hard length spring free. She gave him a filthy grin as she ground down against him, letting him glide along her warm, wet folds. He kissed her, mimicking the roll of his hips with his tongue. She groaned as she slid down, taking him to the hilt. She curled her hand around the back of his neck, rocking against him, growing wetter with every movement.

She tilted her head back, giving him the access he needed to bite and lick at the hollow of her throat. She could feel delicious tension building inside of her and grunted in frustration. She didn't want it to be over just yet. But, she did want Bael's hands on her, and he was blindly tapping his fingertips all over the door.

"Where is the doorknob?" he growled. She laughed, reaching down to open the door.

He walked forward, never slipping out of her. She plucked at the front of his uniform shirt and realized that it didn't button up. She leaned back and pulled at it, but it refused to open. He smirked at her and reached up for the zipper hidden under at the button flap. He lowered the zipper to reveal his white undershirt.

"Sorcery!" she gasped as he walked through the door. She shoved the shirt off of his shoulders and let it drop to the floor. He knelt on the bed, carrying her with him, and the momentum swung the bedframe against the wall. Still kissing her, he glanced up and then he was goggling at the ropes suspending her bed from the ceiling.

He broke away from her mouth. "The hell?"

She nodded as she pushed his pants down his thighs with her feet. "Yeah, my bed swings."

"Interesting." He nipped at her chin, her neck, then between her breasts while she pulled his tank over his head. Pulling away from her, he rose to his knees, dragging her up with him. She took him in hand and slid down the length of him, humming as the hot flesh parted hers.

"That should not feel as good as it does," she sighed, rolling her body against his.

He guided her hips up and down with his hands. And with every thrust, the bed swung and bounced off of the wall.

It sounded just as dirty as it felt.

She could feel his talons sinking into the globes of her ass and the sting only made her pleasure spike higher. She wrapped her arms around his shoulders and clung tighter as his movements sped up. She angled her body so that he ground against just the right spot, sending those lovely little ripples fluttering through her. Bael's hips moved more erratically and the frame knocked against the wall even harder.

She lost track of time and the thumping against the wall. All she could feel was the warmth inside her and pressed against her skin. And when he fell over the edge, dragging her with him, the blossoming heat was less of a shock than it had been the first time.

She went limp against him, barely registering as he laid her gently on the mattress and flopped down next to her.

Jillian turned to press her face to his shoulder and noted the dents in the plaster wall.

"I'm going to lose my security deposit," she panted.

"The town is renting the house, not you."

"Well, the town is going to lose their security deposit. I hope they make you explain why at the next parish commission meeting."

"I'll plead the Fifth," he said, kissing her shoulder.

"As much as I appreciate you popping by for a cup of sex, what was that about?"

"Zed said you got a package from an ex-boyfriend. He said that you were sitting in your van, cooing and cuddling a stuffed animal while stuffing a cupcake into your mouth."

She lifted her head and stared at him. "How the hell would Zed know?"

"Enola overheard you and told his mom, who told Zed, who ran into my office to tell me. I mean, literally ran, with a smile on his face. Because he's an ass."

Jillian slapped at his chest. "So, you came over here because you thought I was cuddling a stuffed animal from my ex-boyfriend? And eating his cupcake? And you thought you would come over here and bang the desire for another man's stuffed animals and cupcakes out of me?"

Bael hesitated and then admitted, "Well, it sounds weird when you put it like that."

"Yeah, the phrasing is the problem."

He rolled over her, pressing her into the mattress "I don't share. This isn't a dragon thing, though my nature definitely doesn't help. But I won't share you with some *drole*."

"I'm not asking you to share. There was a package of cupcakes from my ex-boyfriend, which I didn't want because he's my ex-boyfriend for a reason. I sent them home with Bonita to sugar up her grandchildren. The stuffed animal—" Jillian paused to pick up the plush Drogon from where he'd been shoved aside on the mattress. "Is from my best friend, Sonja, because we haven't been able to binge-watch *Game of Thrones* together while I've been gone. She also sent me her mother's special spice cookies, which is what I was stuffing into my mouth when your not-so-confidential informant spotted me. And I'm not even going to apologize for it, because they're amazing."

"So...no interest in the ex-boyfriend or his cupcakes?"

"No."

"Can I try the spice cookies?"

"No," she told him, rolling and straddling his hips even as he pouted. "Because much like some shifters I know, I don't share."

"Fine."

"How was the public information meeting?"

Bael grimaced. "Some people are mighty scared. Some are taking it in stride. Nobody openly blamed you, if that's what you're worried about."

"I was, a little bit, yeah," she admitted. "So really, neither of us has anything to worry about. You don't have to worry about me accepting cupcakes from other suitors. And I don't have to be worried about being run out of town as murder bait."

"Right, nothing to worry about, except the murders."

"You and your downsides."

He picked up the stuffed dragon. "Cut it out, small fry." And put it on the nightstand, facing away from the bed.

"Why would you do that?"

He pulled her on top of him and kissed her soundly. "Because you already have a dragon in your bed."

12

JILLIAN

Jillian turned her cart down the hot sauce aisle at the Boone Mercantile, looking for presents for Sonja and Mel. She'd decided to send them both care packages of local foods to thank them for the earbud cozies and cookies.

Even with its harsh fluorescent lights, the grocery store was a welcome respite from her kitchen table isolation. She'd spent most of her week writing. Almost every appointment she had for the week was canceled. The subjects were all perfectly polite about it, but they each found some very plausible and unavoidable reason why they couldn't meet with her. It turned out the local people didn't want to be interviewed when people who agreed to interviews turned up dead.

The good news was that the extra time had given her the opportunity to polish her progress report, so the moment her supervisor, Jan Wallace, called demanding an update, Jillian was able to immediately counter the check.

"No problem. I can email it to you by this afternoon. Would you like me to cc the board?" she'd asked.

Jan spluttered on the other end of the line. "Well, don't rush the job. We want careful analysis."

"Oh, I've been keeping notes on my progress the whole time I've been here. Do you not do that when you're in the field?" Jillian's voice was so pointedly guileless, Sonja would have collapsed in giggles to hear it. Because Jan Wallace was a human with a lengthy laundry list of allergies and as long as ragweed existed, she would not be doing field work.

Jillian conceded that this might have been a little mean. She thought maybe she was spending too much time around apex predators. Nevertheless, she'd submitted her report, addressing each of the bullet points Sonja had sent her. And since no one had sent her follow-up questions, Jillian assumed it was satisfactory. Surely Sonja would have sent up a warning flare if it wasn't.

Jillian realized she was standing in the middle of the aisle, staring off into space. She shook off her daze and took two bottles marked DuFrane's Devil Drops with a fire-breathing demon on the label. Mel, who occasionally indulged in gut-destroying spicy food, would love it. Sonja would see it as a challenge, and she never backed down from a challenge.

Due to the wide array of diets among the *magique*, there was a pretty impressive range of products available—everything from Russian caviar to Irish butter. She shuffled along the aisles knocking staples into her cart. With her limited cooking skills, Jillian stuck to sandwiches and cereal. Sonja did most of the cooking at home, out of self-defense. And if Jillian kept getting carry-out from the pie shop when she was in town, she wouldn't be able to button her pants.

She turned into the pasta aisle and ran smack into another cart.

She gasped. "Oh my gosh, I'm so sorry—"

And then she realized mid-sentence that she'd collided with Bael's cousin, Balfour, who was grinning at her with that creepy politician's smile of his. This reminded Jillian that she needed to stop by the cleaning products aisle and pick up a couple of gallons of bleach.

"Miss Ramsay, our northern flower, how are you this fine afternoon?"

Jillian forced her face into a blandly pleasant expression, despite Balfour's refusal to call her, "Dr. Ramsay."

"I'm fine, thank you. And you?"

Balfour tossed his dark hair and stepped closer in what Jillian was sure was meant to be a casual, sexy gesture. She had to suppress the urge to visibly shudder. "Always so polite and formal. I bet you're not so formal with my cousin, now are you? I bet you're real relaxed whenever he's around."

She stared at him for a good long beat. "That's none of your business."

He stepped way too far into her personal space bubble, backing her against the grocery shelf. "Is that what you like about him?" he purred. "That southern drawl of his whispering dirty things into your ear? Or is it his claws? You like him digging those long, sharp claws into your skin, threatening to make you bleed, but not quite?"

She stared at him, her lip curled in disgust, and pictured ramming his face into a frozen side of beef in the meat section.

He reached for a lock of hair that had fallen over her shoulder. "Bael's not the only dragon in town, you know, if that's what you want. I could do all that and more for you."

She pushed his hand away from her and moved away from the grocery shelf. "I wouldn't touch you for all the gold in the parish."

She pushed the cart past him and he caught her arm. "You know, the way things are going in town, I would think you would want to make as many friends as possible. People are starting to think maybe you're bad luck. I could persuade them to think otherwise."

She snorted, thinking of the way Balfour was ignored at Clarissa's party. People might have tolerated Balfour, for his family's sake, but they kept their distance. "I don't think you have nearly as much personal power as you think you do."

He squeezed her arm harder. "Is that what you like? Power?"

"Why do you even care? You've barely spoken two words to me since I arrived in town and I haven't done *anything* to give you the impression I'm interested." She realized she was whispering, preventing a scene, which only served to protect Balfour, so she raised her voice to add, "Back off."

"But I want to know what makes you tick. I want to know what happens inside your head to make you do the things you do."

She yanked her arm away from him, then reached into her bag to flip the switch on Bael's Taser. "Stay away from me. Don't come near me. Don't come near my house. Don't talk to me. Don't even think of me."

His grin seemed to have more teeth than she remembered. His eyes flashed a sickly yellow as he lowered his mouth near her ear. "And what are you going to do to stop me?"

She pulled the Taser out of her bag, fully charged, and blindly shoved it at his crotch. Balfour's eyes went wide and he turned just in time for her to catch his hip instead of zipper. She pulled the trigger and the contacts fired. He shrieked, jerking and flailing before collapsing on the floor.

"I'll do that," she said, stepping over his twitching body and continued on to the next aisle.

Her face burned as she walked away from her full cart, realizing that the dozen or so shoppers in the store were staring at her. Let them stare. She hadn't done anything wrong. She hadn't over-reacted. And if they didn't want dragons having full body seizures in their grocery store aisle, maybe they needed better store security.

Jillian sighed, remembering her expectations were too high. Also, she just remembered that Balfour's family owned the grocery store where she'd Tased him.

She was going to have to start going to the Walmart in Slidell.

She was shaking by the time she reached the door. She had a cold sinking dread of what was behind her, that if she turned back she would find Balfour running at her, claws and fangs ready. Just as Jillian reached the sidewalk, a hand closed around her shoulder and she shrieked. She whirled around with the depleted Taser in hand, because smacking Balfour in the face with it would work.

Simon Malfater held his hands in a defensive posture. "Don't shoot!"

"Simon," she gasped. "I'm so sorry. I just—"

He smiled, patting her on the shoulder. "I know, I saw. I just wanted to make sure you're all right. Balfour can be a little aggressive sometimes. I don't think he realizes his own strength."

"I don't think he cares about his strength."

Simon chuckled. "There's that, too. Can I walk you to your car?"

She didn't want to be that girl, the one who needs some man to protect her from the consequences of confronting an asshole. But at the same time, there was a good chance that her adrenaline would drain away and her legs would collapse underneath her if she tried to cross the parking lot without the buddy system.

"Thank you, that would be very thoughtful of you."

He smiled warmly. "Aw, no problem, *cher*. If you're feeling shaky, I could drive you home."

"Jillian?"

Still holding Simon's arm, she turned toward the voice shouting her name and saw Bael running full-tilt down Main

Street in his uniform. Simon's hand was whipped away from her while Bael scooped her up and carried her almost half a block away.

"Ooof," she wheezed. "Bael, what are you doing?"

He stopped running at the sound of her voice, wrapping her legs around him and supporting her butt with his hands.

"Junior Claymore was in the market, buyin' fish fry. He called my office, told Theresa that Balfour tried to hurt you." He leaned back, looking her over for injuries.

"I will never get used to the *magie* grapevine system," she muttered into his shoulder as he carried her back toward the store. "He didn't really try to hurt me. He barely touched me. He just kept asking what it was about you that I liked, telling me that he could do that and more for me. He was just creepy and aggressive. Clearly, he learned how to flirt from Charles Manson."

Bael glared at the door to the grocery. Balfour was standing just behind the glass doors, smirking at his cousin. Bael set her gently on her feet, though his expression was thunderous. Jillian pressed her hands to his chest and, despite the fact that she'd planted her feet, Bael just kept walking toward the door, sliding Jillian's sneakers across the pavement. "Bael, don't. It's not worth it, causing a public scene. It will only make things worse with your grandfather."

She pushed her shoulder into his chest as she scrambled against the blacktop. "Bael! Please, I just want to go home."

Then Bael glared at Balfour, while wrapping an arm around Jillian. "All right. I'm sorry. Come on, sweetheart. I'll drive you home."

Jillian turned to Simon. "Thanks for your help, Simon.

"Any time," Simon said, shrugging his shoulders.

"I haven't forgotten about interviewing you. I'll give you a call soon, OK?"

Simon grinned and waved at her as Bael opened the passenger door of the van and lifted Jillian into the seat.

Bael opened the driver's side door and held his hand out for the keys. "You're coming to my place. You're going to stay with me."

"Rephrase, please?" she told him. "Also, why do none of my invitations to people's homes include the words 'please' or 'you have the option'?"

"I would feel better if you stayed with me while there is a murderer on the loose. And Balfour."

"Have you considered that Balfour is a suspect in those murders?"

"What, why?"

"Because he's creepy and he doesn't respect personal space. And some of the comments he's made. He scares me, Bael."

"Balfour's all right. He just doesn't understand how to... people. He doesn't understand why I'm with you."

"Hey."

"You're human. And he knows that means I could suffer consequences with my family, but I'm choosing to be with you anyway. And to him that means that you have some sort of secret that he needs to find out."

"So you're locking me up in a vault. Like a princess. In a tower. That you're guarding. Like a dragon."

"I'm not trying to lock you up in a vault. I treasure you. But you're not my treasure. I know that."

Jillian pressed her lips together in a frown.

"I will sleep better at night, if I know you're safe. And you know how important it is for me to sleep at night, with my dangerous and fast-paced job."

"Zed said you only wrote one ticket last week. And it was to Zed."

"Do you want to see a dragon pout? Because I will lower myself to pouting. For you."

She crossed her arms over her chest. "Fine, but I'm bringing my stuffed dragon."

"I am going to burn that thing."

"You wouldn't dare," she shot back. "Also, for the record, I consider Zed a suspect."

"What?"

She threw up her hands. "I don't trust anyone who is that consistently cheerful."

"Zed would be hurt by that. He and his mother have practically adopted you."

"Fine, but I'm still going to keep an eye on him," she said.

Bael's house looked completely normal from the outside, a two-story brick Georgian style with white shutters. It was pretty big for one person, but Zed had mentioned to Jillian that most of the Boones lived in mini-mansions around town. By comparison, he was living modestly.

She tugged her laptop onto her shoulder while Bael grabbed her duffel from the backseat. She supposed she should be grateful that he'd stopped by her house so she could pick up more clothes. Also, she didn't have any groceries in her house, so she hoped Bael stocked up at some point.

Bael's house was more subtly decorated than she'd expected. There were no golden dragons mounted on the walls or gem-studded faucets. The furniture was sturdy and comfortable, covered in cream colored fabrics with touches of forest green and gold. His back porch opened onto the Fool's Blood River, so she could hear the water rushing, even through the closed doors. She noted that Zed and Bael and Clarissa occupied most of the photo frames, though there were a few black and white shots of a younger couple, wearing styles from the 1940s. The woman had Bael's straight, slim nose and the man smiled Bael's warm smile. They had to be his parents. And the toddler perched on his mother's knee had to be Bael. In the 1940s. She was dating a Baby Boomer.

Bael led her down the hallway, with its dark hardwood floors, and opened the bedroom door. Jillian's jaw dropped. The room was windowless and cavernous. The ceilings had to be twenty feet high, at least, and the room itself took up more than half the house. A huge nest of pillows was situated in the center of the room, but there was no other furniture. Not even a night stand.

"Your bedroom is huge," she noted. "And you have no bed."

"It's a dragon thing. But I promise, it's plenty comfortable."

"I have no doubt. But keep in mind, if you're going to keep me here, you're going to have to feed me," she told him.

"Not a problem. Clarissa packs up meals for me every week, 'so I don't starve to death.' You want reheated meatloaf or reheated gumbo?" he asked.

She laughed. "You have that woman wrapped around your little finger."

"It's kind of like when a tiger adopts a baby goat at the zoo. It's unnatural and shouldn't warm your heart, and yet it does."

And so they proceeded to spend a very pleasant evening, at home, eating reheated meatloaf and watching old movies. There were no interruptions, no discussion of murder. Bael ignored several texts from Zed asking why Balfour came to his office demanding justice for his nearly electrocuted balls.

For just a night, it was nice to pretend they had a regular relationship without inter-species tension or possible serial killers. And falling asleep on a giant pile of pillows was much easier than she anticipated. Before she drifted off, her face pressed against Bael's shoulder, she couldn't think of a single thing she needed to do the next day. Instead of her usual habit of constructing a to-do list, her mind simply went quiet and slipped into a pleasant darkness.

Around 2 a.m., Jillian woke up very warm, so warm that she'd sweat through her clothes. She kicked off her blankets and sat up, wondering if she should open a window. Instead of the firm feather mattress she'd become accustomed to, she felt warm, smooth skin.

The body was immense, far too large to be a person, and covered in scales as seamless as glass. She blinked, shaking the last traces of sleep away from her head. And then she shook her head because she didn't believe what she was seeing, a huge gold and green dragon wrapped around her like a faithful hound. She was cradled in a soft leathery wing, pressed against the dragon's warm belly. Her foot was wedged against the dragon's horned snout. She quickly drew back her foot, as if the dragon would wake and suddenly decide to take off a few of her toes.

She supposed this was why his bedroom was so large. In his dragon form, he could barely curl himself inside this room. If he changed forms in his sleep, he wouldn't want to take out a wall. Sliding off of the wing, she crouched in front of the dragon's head, which was the size of a smart car.

The scales on his face were bright, glowing gold, with green showing around the edges of each tiny circle. Spiky green growths like claws grew from his brow and ran in symmetrical rows down his snout. She traced the slopes of his nose with her fingertips, marveling how he could stand to run so hot all the time. He was like a living furnace.

He was the most beautiful thing she'd ever seen. And he was Bael.

The eye, glowing from within like a living topaz, snapped open and focused on her. She clutched her fingers to her chest and scrambled back. Bael shook his head like a dog throwing off water.

"Don't panic," she told herself. "Don't panic. It's still Bael."

His forked tongue flicked out, tasting the air like a snake. It snapped playfully across the bridge of her foot, and then wound around her ankle, pulling her closer to him. He nuzzled his nose at her knees and then at her side, all the while flicking that tongue against her skin.

The flush of arousal she felt was as alarming as it was complete. She wanted Bael, badly. She spread her palms along his snout.

"OK, Bael, I need you to go back to your human form, because there are some things even I'm not open-minded enough to try."

His body shrank into itself, still golden and glowing, until it was just Bael. His mouth crashed down on hers like an ocean wave, all tongue and clacking teeth.

"You're really pretty when you're a dragon," she told him.

"No one has ever said that to me before." He kissed her again, his claws tearing at the sides of her panties.

She bit lightly at his chin, making him growl. "Do me a favor when we go back to sleep. Don't roll over."

13

BAEL

Bael and Jillian established a routine over the next few weeks. As the community relaxed back into normalcy and people forgot about the horrors that Ted and Gladys had suffered, they became more willing to talk to Jillian. She rescheduled the canceled interviews, collected questionnaires and entered data into spreadsheets.

Most afternoons, she got back to Bael's house before his shift was over and had something either reheated or assembled from ready-mixes before he got home. They'd eat, talk about their days. Sometimes Zed came over, and he and Bael watched sports while Jillian worked. And then, when Zed left, they'd attempt to shred Bael's pillow bed with some bone-bending sex.

He enjoyed making her part of his routine. He'd been alone for so long that he'd forgotten what it was like to come home to someone, to call out when he opened his door and know they would answer. He'd forgotten what it was like to have a home, instead of just having a house.

There were bumps along the way. They could not agree on appropriate television volume. Bael took way too long in the shower, in Jillian's opinion, for someone who had very little hair to wash. And one morning, Jillian woke up glowing, literally.

Bael had been sleeping when she discovered the issue. He'd woken up to her shrieking, "What the hell is this?!"

Jillian's entire body was glowing. She was a beacon of golden light in the dark room. Frowning, Bael scrubbed a hand across the back of his head. "Yeah, I probably should have mentioned that."

She scowled at him. "Mentioned what?"

He cleared his throat. "Sometimes, when a dragon takes on a human partner, well, after the exchange of...my contribution... you take a little bit of my fire into you. And you glow. It's supposed to draw me even closer to you. You know, the whole 'dragons are attracted to shiny objects,' thing?"

"Your body fluids are going to make me bioluminescent?"

"Not permanently," he assured her.

"Oh, well, that's a comfort." She stared down at her glowing form. "So, I won't get pregnant."

"No."

"But I'm going to glow in the dark?"

"There are women who pay top dollar for this sort of thing!" he exclaimed.

"Are you telling me there's dragon semen in high-end beauty products?"

"No, it's more of an internal process...Never mind."

She glowered at him. "How long until I can leave the house?"

"You've never been more beautiful to me." He tried to smile his most charming smile, but she was not having it.

"How long?!"

"A few days," he admitted.

She poked her finger into his warm chest. "I am going to call Zed and have him gnaw on you."

"That seems fair."

While she'd been grumpy about her seclusion, Jillian eventually admitted she was grateful for her "indoors time." It gave her an excuse to focus solely on her work. And she also seemed to enjoy the offerings of chocolate and beignets Bael brought her to make up for his not saying anything about the glowing semen... And to prevent her from following through on her threat to tell Zed. The shit he would have given Bael would have been thorough and relentless.

It was bad enough that Zed came into his office to "officially rebuke" him. He wore a tie and everything. It was clipped on to his t-shirt, but it was still pretty clear Zed was wearing his Mayor hat and not his friend hat.

"So, we gotta talk," Zed said, tugging at his shirt collar. "There's been a complaint about your job performance."

"In terms of?"

"We have two unsolved murders and people are scared."

"Someone actually filed a complaint, saying 'I'm scared?'" Bael asked.

"No, they said that you're incompetent and that if you're going to try to do a thankless human job, you should at least do it well so you don't embarrass yourself."

Bael frowned. He'd heard those exact words come out of someone's mouth. "*Balfour* filed a complaint about me?"

"You know I can't say." But Zed was nodding. "In an unrelated note, your cousin's an asshole."

Bael rolled his eyes. At least he knew that the complaint was filed by someone who didn't really count. Balfour had always held a grudge against Bael, and now he was just taking advantage of the situation. If Bael somehow got fired from his "thankless human job," it would mean even more loss of face with their grandfather.

But still, if Balfour was filing a complaint, that had to mean there was some rumbling of disapproval from Mystic Bayou's residents. Balfour never did anything unless he thought he could get away with it.

"For the record, Jillian thinks Balfour killed Gladys and Ted."

Zed scoffed. "Really? I mean, as I said, he's an asshole. But I can't see him killing anybody. Why would he do it?"

"To make me look bad? Make everybody afraid under my watch? The more I think about it, the less insane it sounds. But until there's some evidence that he had anything to do with it, my hands are tied. So now what?" Bael asked.

"I've officially put you on notice. You are hereby rebuked," Zed told him. "Now, you ignore it. You just keep doing what you're doing. You know the job. Sometimes, stuff comes up and you can't control it and all you can do is work your way through it."

Bael grumbled.

"Did you get any information back from the League's forensic people?" Zed asked.

"A whole lot of nothing. There were no fingerprints on the doors besides Gladys and Ted's. No foreign DNA on the swabs I took near the wounds. They were able to tell me that the perp used a very sharp knife, to which I say, 'no shit.'"

"Well, the chances of them finding some *CSI*, 'this bat guano is only found in a two-square mile section of the swamp,' key to everything was pretty unlikely. I hate to say it, but all we can do is watch people for any odd behaviors."

"Well, please don't tell Jillian. It'd probably hurt her feelings if I called her coworkers basically useless."

"How's all that goin'?" Zed grinned. "You still got her locked away in your tower?"

"Why does everybody keep mentioning a tower? There's no tower!" Bael exclaimed.

"Aw, hell, I think it's sweet that you two are all shacked up.

You've been sixty-percent less of a grumpy bastard since she started sleeping over. You thinking about making it permanent?"

Bael's mouth quirked at the corners. He had in fact, been thinking about making their arrangement permanent. He wanted marriage and hatchlings and the whole nine yards. He didn't care about his grandfather's wrath or the possibility of losing out on his share of the family hoard. While he'd wanted to honor his father's wishes, Bael knew his father would rather see him happy than richer.

He just didn't know how to approach Jillian about it. He'd shown her his hoard and her response was, "That's nice, for science!" Bael's father had shown Bael's mother his hoard and she'd practically swooned.

He was going to have to get more creative.

"Uh, Bael, you've been staring off into the distance and smiling all weird for the last five minutes."

Bael snickered. "Sorry."

"You don't look sorry."

Bael's reply was interrupted by Theresa's appearance in Bael's office doorway. Her expression was stricken and her complexion was nearly gray. Zed glanced up and muttered, "Aw, shit."

14

JILLIAN

Hours later, long after the sun rose on a new day, Bael unlocked his door to find Jillian

perched on his kitchen chair, one leg tucked under the other as she read. There was a pencil in her mouth and a red pen stuck through her twisted hair. A cup of coffee sat forgotten near her elbow. She looked up, her eyes slightly unfocused, and grinned at him...until she saw the expression on his face.

"Another one?" she sighed. He nodded. She rose from her chair and wrapped her arms around his shoulders.

"Teenie Clackston."

"I hadn't met her yet."

"You didn't have an appointment with her?" Bael asked.

Jillian shook her head, a relieved expression on her face.

"She was a sweet woman who made blackberry wine and brought it down to city hall every Christmas. I used to tease her about arresting her for running an unlicensed brewing operation, but the wine was so damn good, I couldn't stand to. She was a room mom for her daughter's second grade class, for gold's sake.

Her husband... Her poor husband is heartbroken. And I don't know what to tell him."

"I'm so sorry, Bael. I was worried when you didn't come home last night, but I figured something had come up. Was Teenie human?

"You know that doesn't matter to me, I'd mourn her either way."

"No, I know. I'm just curious. Was she human or shifter? I think you mentioned her before."

"She was born human, but about ten years ago, she developed these supernatural skills in the kitchen. Soups that could actually cure the common cold. Cakes that could soothe a broken heart. For New Year's, she'd do a big crawfish boil and wish everybody good fortune. And somehow, everybody who showed up had better luck. Zed's already talking about putting on a big memorial for her on New Year's. He'll probably ask you for help organizing something classy."

She tilted her head. "I probably won't be here for New Year's."

"Do you already have plans? Are you gonna visit your parents for the holidays?"

"No, but I'll probably be gone by next month. You knew this isn't a permanent assignment, right? When I'm done, I move onto the next study. After taking such a big assignment on the fly, I should have my choice of field studies, especially if my report goes over well."

"So you're just going to leave when you're finished? Even with what's between us? You wormed your way into our community and you're just going to leave?"

"I think I resent the word 'wormed,' but yes, that's my job. Look, I feel for you... The things I feel for you, I've never felt for anyone else. But I can't give you the whole white picket dragon's lair and nest full of eggs."

"What is wrong with that?"

"Nothing, it's just not for me. I worked really hard for my career. It's my passion in life. And I'm not going to apologize for wanting to keep it."

"Well, I've waited decades for my mate to come 'round and I'm not going to apologize for wanting to keep her."

"You can't keep me. I'm not one of your treasures. I'm a person."

"We've gone over this, Jillian. I don't want to keep you with my treasures. That's the whole reason I took you to my hoard. Don't you understand what that means?"

"You trusted me not to steal it."

"No, it means, I have real, life-altering feelings for you. It means I see you as a potential mate. It means I want to show you that I can provide for you, that this isn't just a quick roll on the coins. It's pretty much a marriage proposal."

She stared at him, mouth gaping like a beached fish.

"Well, how the hell am I supposed to know that?" she exclaimed. "This is the problem with you dragons being so secretive. You can't deny humans information about your culture and then get mad at us for misunderstanding. That's why I want to keep working, to help people with relationships like ours, to help them understand how Mystic Bayou works!"

"Mystic Bayou works because we make it work. That's the problem with 'your study.' You're trying to show people how to duplicate how we live here, and you can't."

"Why not?"

"Because what we have here is special!" Bael exclaimed.

"I'm not going to deny that. But there are other special towns out there that could be just as great."

"So you're trying to franchise Mystic Bayou, like *magie* McDonald's? I'm not supposed to be bothered by that?"

Jillian threw her hands up. "Why are you trying to twist my words?"

"Why are you trying to ruin my town?" he shot back, dropping his case files on the table with a *thwack.*

"What are you talking about? I'm not trying to ruin anything. I'm just trying to help people!" she cried, pausing as a plastic bag containing a blood-smeared piece of paper fluttered out of Bael's files and to the floor.

"What's this?" she asked, bending to pick it up.

"Zed found it on the floor of Gladys's kitchen. We're assuming it belonged to the killer. It's just a page full of crazy."

"That's not crazy. It's short hand. Every scientist I know has their own way of writing notes. The killer's writing his observations down. Don't you do that with your investigation notes?"

"I record mine in a voice recorder and transcribe it later. More precise that way," he said.

The corner of her mouth lifted as she examined the page.

Bael asked. "What was he observing?"

"I have no idea," she said. "Everybody's short hand is different, personal. Maybe if you had a handwriting sample from everybody in town and a crazy person conversion chart, I could help you, but I can't decipher this."

Bael dropped into a kitchen chair and rubbed his hands over his head. Jillian breathed deeply and opened his files to look at the crime scene photos. It took a lot of pauses and patience, but she flipped through all of them.

"Bael, were there any accidental deaths before Ted turned up dead? Any deaths that were attributed to drowning or animal attacks or just disappearances?"

"I know how to do my job, Jillian."

"I know you do, I'm just wondering if there were any deaths that didn't feel right to you. Where there was more damage to the body than there should have been. Because this just doesn't feel like a serial killer."

"How do you mean?"

"Now that I can stand to look at them, I see that all of the cuts seem almost surgical. These aren't angry crimes."

"So, what you're a forensic analyst now? Not all serial killers are angry. I think you've been watching too much TV."

"I'm not a forensics expert. I'm a people expert. And when I'm learning about a culture, I look at commonalities. What keeps a group together? What do they have in common? Ted, Gladys, and Teenie, they were different types of *magique*. They were different ages and genders. They had different jobs, moved in different social circles. They believed in different gods. They had no family connections, which in itself is a miracle in this town. What do they have in common?"

"They weren't born *magique*," he replied. "They were changed by the rift."

"And what if these killings aren't murder for murder's sake, but because this person wants to understand how the victims work, like they're specimens? He doesn't consider them murders. They're dissections."

"That would be incredibly upsetting."

He pulled out a map of the bayou and marked the rift with a big red X.

"Where was Ted Beveux's house?" she asked.

Bael leaned over the map and circled Ted's house. It was one of the closest homes in town to the rift. "Gladys's house is right here."

He circled another spot on the map, which was just slightly farther out from the rift. Without being prompted, he circled what she assumed was Teenie's house, which was only a little bit farther from the big red X. He marked another spot, which looked to be just outside of the "*magique* only" line near the rift.

"We had a boating accident a couple years ago right here. The bodies were torn up, but we thought they'd been picked at by scavengers. It was a pair of teenage brothers. They'd just started developing what we thought was lycanthropy. And here, we had a little girl who drowned in a creek. Sarah Winters, she'd been born a natural healer in a family where there were no *magique*."

"He's working his way out from the rift, taking apart people who have turned."

Bael gathered his files back into the laptop bag. "I gotta go talk to Zed, see if there are any other cases we're missing. I want you to stay here. Don't leave. Don't answer the door unless it's for me, Zed or Clarissa. Don't even answer your phone. I'm going to pull the van into the garage so no one knows you're home."

"Bael, we just talked about this."

"You're going to stay here with my guns and my heavily locked doors. I know you're not a treasure to be hoarded. You're a person. And I know things are messed up right now, but you're *my* person. I'm asking as someone who feels for you. I'm begging you to stay somewhere it's safe."

"Oh, that is not fair."

He kissed her, all fury and fear, and she sagged against him in relief.

"Fine, I'll stay here."

"Thank you. I'll bring you home a pie."

"You know, pie doesn't solve everything."

"You'd be surprised."

15

JILLIAN

Jillian thought it had been stressful to present her doctoral thesis in front of some of the world's foremost experts in her field. It turned out that was nothing compared to waiting around for your dragon-cop boyfriend to call and tell you whether he caught a serial killer.

She did every bit of work she could conjure up. She organized her files. She cleaned the house. She even tried cooking, only to throw away the chicken she'd burned. Nothing would calm her nerves. So she took to pacing in the living room, running over all of the possibilities in her head and coming up with nothing definite.

This didn't make any sense. Why take apart your neighbors when you could just ask them questions? What could make you so unhappy that you committed murder for the sake of knowledge? That you killed children? Had the rift driven the killer crazy?

She heard a car door slam and went to the window, expecting to see Bael. But instead of a squad car, she saw a large red pick-up truck parked in the driveway. Balfour was taking a bag out of the passenger seat and walking toward the house. She ran to the front door and double checked the lock. She watched Balfour move closer to the window.

If Balfour really wanted to get in, he would. Bael's boat was tied to the back dock. Could she pilot it away before Balfour figured out how close she was? Would he only shift into dragon form and chase her down? Regardless, running seemed better than staying, better than being cornered.

Balfour spotted her through the front window and smirked. She grabbed her purse and slipped out the back door. She backed down the length of the porch, listening as Balfour jerked the door handle.

The little fishing boat was only a few steps away. She just had to work up the nerve to take her eyes off of the house. She backed toward the dock. She heard a footstep behind her and didn't even have time to turn her head before a great weight came crashing against her temple. Her legs folded under her and she saw the briefest flash of sky overhead before her eyelids fluttered closed.

SHE WOKE up face down on a dirt floor in a shed, which was bad. Her hands were cuffed behind her back and there was duct tape over her mouth, which was worse.

She wriggled, trying to get control of her limbs so she could pull up to an upright position. Her hands and feet felt numb. And there was a ringing in her ears that was distinctly unpleasant. Her head ached with a dull, gnawing throb. She'd been crying and her nose was stuffy, making it hard to breathe.

The shed was small but meticulously organized. There was a surgical table in the corner. And she recognized several medical tools on a metal tray. There were anatomical sketches all over the walls and photos of dissections. She recognized several of the symbols from the notes he'd left at the scene, but she still couldn't figure out what any of them meant.

The corner of the tape at her mouth was loose. She nudged her face against her shoulder, slowly and painfully peeling it away from her skin. When she was finally free, she sucked in huge gulping mouthfuls of air.

Bael. She wanted Bael. She just wanted to see his face again. She wanted to tell him she loved him and she was sorry she made him feel like he wasn't as important as her work. Her eyes welled up and she couldn't tell if it was from heartbreak or panic or the result of being knocked unconscious. It probably didn't matter. She just wanted Bael.

Also, she wanted her Swiss Army knife. But she couldn't see her purse anywhere. The creep who bashed her over her head must have hidden it somewhere.

She heard footsteps outside. Should she pretend to be unconscious again? Would it be better if she could surprise him in case he uncuffed her? She was still mulling over her options when Simon Malfater, the sweet unassuming science teacher from the joint school, walked into the shed.

"Oh, for the love of fuck," she muttered, shattering any hope she had of pretending to sleep. She felt like such an idiot. Of course it was Simon. He was a scientist. He would have no trouble taking a life form apart to understand how it worked.

Simon was with her when she'd spoken to Ted about their interview. He was at the grocery store when she ran afoul of Balfour, and even offered to drive her home. What would he have done if she'd agreed? If Bael hadn't intercepted them?

"I know. Surprise," Simon drawled. "I sat outside the sheriff's house for days, waiting for you to come out on your own. If I knew it would take Balfour approaching your door, I would have called him days ago."

"Balfour, is he in on this?"

He scoffed. "No, he's just a useful tool. All I had to do is ask him a few questions about you, make points about how interested Bael seemed in you. It was like winding up a little toy soldier, sending it after you."

"So, not a murderer, just a creep." She sighed. "I don't know if that makes it better or worse."

Simon snorted. "You know what I find insulting about all this? No one even considered me. Sheriff Boone hasn't questioned me. No one asked me where I was when my subjects met their end. Hell, you never even followed up on your half-hearted offer to interview me. I don't know why you even bothered pretending that you were interested."

"I *was* interested. I *am*, I *am* interested. I wanted all perspectives on what it's like to live here."

Simon sneered. "You want my perspective? It's bullshit. It's all bullshit. A promise that never gets fulfilled. I grew up being nothing special in a town full of extraordinary. And I figured that was my lot, because I was human. And then all these other humans started getting gifts. And I wondered why not me? I deserve it. I wanted it more. And you, you just brought it all into focus for me. Ted was just wasting his life, scaring teenagers and tourists, stirring up trouble. Gladys secretly hated what she was, she didn't appreciate it. She was trying to find a cure. Teenie could have helped so many people, but she kept it to a select few. They wasted the gifts that they were given. So I took them back, to earn mine. But no matter what I did, I couldn't figure out why they were chosen. I was humane. I followed protocols. I knocked them out with chloroform before I started the dissections. But I didn't get any reward for my efforts. No answers. Why them and not me? There is nothing special about them, nothing special inside them. All unremarkable. And that was what was most maddening of all. And you weren't even born here, you just showed up. Why would you get chosen?"

"I think there's been some sort of mistake," she told him. "I'm not a shifter."

Simon's face flushed an angry red, his eyes darkening. "Don't lie to me. Don't treat me like I'm stupid. I'm just as smart as you are, even if I didn't go to all those fancy schools. I've seen the glow in you, over the last few weeks, that magic that only comes from being a shifter."

She sighed, closing her eyes. If she lived through this, she was going to get Bael fixed. It would take a huge lampshade collar, but she could get one from the League. She pulled at the cuffs behind her, which felt pretty solid. Maybe if she kept him talking, it would give Bael time to find her.

"Or it can be a sign that you're sleeping with one. Apparently, having sex with a dragon leaves you with glowing skin. It's a mating thing. It's supposed to keep Bael interested in me."

"Liar. It's a shifter trait."

"Look, I know it sounds like a cop-out, but dragons don't share much about their culture. I didn't know it was happening either until Bael explained it to me. I'm not a shifter. I'm not any kind of *magie*. I'm just like you, a human, a scientist."

He yanked her to her feet, pulling her toward the dissection table. "Is that what they taught you to do at the League? To find common ground with your subjects during interviews? Well, don't bother. I tried finding common ground with them, too, and it didn't work. They were nothing like me. And you're not either."

He uncuffed her hands long enough to shackle her hands to the dissection table. While he was trying to close the cuff around her wriggling wrist, she reached toward the surgical tray and grabbed a scalpel. "Stop struggling," he growled. "This is going to happen! You should feel fortunate. You're the first one I've ever brought to my research facility. This time, I'm going to have all of my tools at my disposal. This time, it's going to work!"

"No!" she yelled, jerking her sore arm up and jabbing the scalpel toward his neck. Unfortunately, he moved his arm up to shield himself and she caught him in the bicep. But the pain was enough to get him to let go of her arms. Simon dropped to his knees, screaming, though a tiny blade to the arm couldn't have been nearly as painful as what he'd put his victims through. She screamed, jerking her shackled arm away from the surgical table. The wooden strut holding the shackles to the metal table shattered and the shackle came swinging toward her head.

"No!" Simon seethed. He grabbed a scalpel that had dropped to the ground and slashed it across her belly.

Yowling in pain, Jillian brought the broken wooden strut down on his head, knocking him to the side as she ran for the shed door. She threw her shoulder against it and it gave way beneath the force of her adrenaline, leaving her in the purple twilight of the bayou. Gasping for breath, Jillian propped her hands on her knees and focused on staying upright. The shed was situated by a dock, both of them behind a perfectly nice, normal-looking house on the water. The lawn was neatly kept. There was a ceramic goose on the back porch, for Heaven's sake.

Simon lurched into the doorway, his head bleeding. "You bitch. I'll tie you down and take you apart while you're still awake."

"You snuck up on me once. It won't happen again. You think Bael is scary? I deal with *grant committees*! I'll destroy a little worm like you."

And in the distance, there came a roar.

All of the blood drained from Simon's face. Jillian turned to see a massive golden beast with green-gold wings and green ridges on his back. She screamed out of sheer joy at the sight of him. Bael roared, a ball of flame belching out of his throat and heading straight for Simon.

Simon grabbed her shoulders and shoved her into the line of

the fire, catching her shirt. The flames licked up her arms. She beat away the flames with her hands as she ran from Simon, heading for the house. Simon was running down the dock in the direction of his boat. She tripped, and decided to roll on the grass to extinguish the flames. Maybe it was the adrenaline, but she couldn't even feel the heat. It didn't hurt. It just smelled like burning cotton.

Bael landed on two feet in front of Jillian, pulling her to her feet. He was naked, but there was a gun strapped to his ankle with a very stretchy elastic material. "Are you all right?"

"What are you doing?" she cried. "Get back into your dragon form!"

"Are you all right?" he asked again, checking her arms for burns. "Jillian, honey, are you OK?"

"I'm fine!" she cried as he bent to take his gun from his ankle. "Just get him!"

Simon's boat engine roared to life. She watched as Bael ran down the length of the dock, his naked cheeks bouncing, as Simon's boat pulled away into the swamp. Bael raised and emptied his gun, firing at the boat, hitting the outboard motor a few times, but only glancing Simon's shoulder. Simon howled, clutching his hand at the wound.

Somehow, that pissed Jillian off even more than the whole "tried to kill her" part. He'd cut people apart, nice people with lives of their own, and Simon couldn't take a little shoulder wound.

Jillian ran to join Bael as the boat pulled farther away into the murky waters. "Just turn into a dragon and burn him!"

Bael sighed. "I can't."

As the fuel poured out of the boat, the motor died, leaving Simon drifting across the black water. "No, really, I believe you can cross the distance. Look, he's right there, ripe for the immolation."

Standing on unsteady feet, Simon leaned over the motor and tried to start the engine. His hands were slick with blood and he made several false pulls on the cable, letting it slip from his fingers.

"Jillian, that's not the right way."

"What do you mean? You nearly fried the guy just a few minutes ago!"

"That was the dragon seeing his mate in danger. Now I'm the sheriff and he's a perpetrator who needs to face justice. I need to make an arrest, by the book. I can't put, 'And I decided to burn him alive because he hurt my girlfriend.'"

"So, you're going to do what? Send him to state prison, where he's going to blab all of Mystic Bayou's secrets to the other inmates? Do you really want *that* to be the reason your secrets are exposed to the world?"

"Maybe. Maybe the state'll decide that he's too crazy to be held in the general population and send him to a hospital where he'll get the help he needs."

"Now is not the time to debate the merits of the criminal justice system!" she yelled.

"I just don't want you to see me kill a man, okay?"

She threw her hands up. "I'm telling you now, I'm okay with it!"

Jillian watched a dark shape moving in the water, circling closer to the boat. Simon swayed on his feet, blood leaking down his arms. He leaned out over the water as he tried to beat life into the engine.

"Bael, I really think you need to get over there."

"It's fine. It's not like he's going to be able to start the boat with his engine all busted up like that."

Suddenly, a ten-foot alligator lunged up from the water, snapping its jaws around Simon's head. His torso flailed pitifully as he was dragged under the water. A geyser of blood and bubbles exploded from the bottom, and Jillian covered her mouth with her hands, swallowing a scream.

"Well, shit," Bael muttered.

Jillian's mouth was still hanging open, unable to produce sound.

"Are you all right?" he asked and she nodded.

"This is going to be hard to explain to my bosses," she sighed as he hugged her tight.

"Your bosses? I'm the one who let a serial killer get eaten by a gator. That is not how you win elections."

She hissed at a hot, bright pain in her middle, pulling away from him. They watched as the slash across her stomach knitted itself back together. Now it was Bael's turn to stare.

"Is this because of you?" she asked. "From spending too much time with you? The whole glowing semen thing?"

"I'm sure that's it," Bael told her carefully.

He pressed her to his chest, hand cradling her head. "Everything is going to be all right," he promised her. "Every single thing."

16

BAEL

Weeks later, Bael closed the cover of Jillian's bound report. The crazy woman had written a damn textbook while she was living in Miss Lottie's funny little house.

Then again, textbooks had never made him smile so much. "Mystic Bayou: A Whole-Hearted Approach to a Blended Community" was an academic work, complete with graphs and footnotes on all the cultural points people considered vital. But it was also heartfelt, funny and presented the locals in a loving, generous light. Hell, she might have given his neighbors more credit than they deserved.

The study was dedicated to the memories of Ted, Gladys and Teenie, and included a chapter on emotional alienation of human subjects living amongst the *magique*. She addressed Simon's case, specifically, and discussed how experts might be able to help humans living amongst the *magique* adjust to life without special gifts. He wasn't surprised that she'd turned something scary, something that had hurt her directly into an opportunity to help other people.

She'd been agonizingly polite when she thanked him for saving her from Simon, but somehow, a distance had grown between them in the time her knife wound healed to Zed arriving on the scene to help him clean things up. She'd gotten a ride home from Clarissa, then she locked herself in Miss Lottie's house during her last days in the Bayou. Then she promptly left town to present her work to her bosses.

Zed and Clarissa had wanted to throw her a going-away party. But after everything the town had been through, Jillian wanted to leave quietly.

Bael had made the decision to stay away, to let her leave, and to let her have her career, if that was going to make her happy. He loved her with everything in his heart, but he didn't want to keep her with him if it meant she was miserable. So he'd kept to his house, taken sick days and done all the paperwork for Simon's case from home.

When she didn't show up to say goodbye, he figured that was all he needed to know.

"Would you stop poring over that thing? It's not like there's a secret code inside for 'what Jillian is thinking?' Just call the woman!" Zed had been sitting in Bael's office chair and Bael didn't even realize it. And given the self-satisfied look on his face, he'd been there for a while.

"I wouldn't have given you that copy if I knew you were going to obsess over it."

Bael laid the book carefully on his desk. "I just wanted to see what all of the fuss was about. I can't help but notice she talks about the rift and its influence on the locals in detail. You're really gonna let the League know about it?"

"I think we're going to have to. We need League resources to determine how quickly the rift's energy is changing and what, if anything, can be done to slow down its progression."

"That's gonna mean more scientists. More League personnel."

"Yeah, and it could mean that a certain League scientist could come back."

17

JILLIAN

Across the country, Jillian twitched as she waited in the plush waiting room of the League's D.C. offices. Even with the expensive looking tooled leather chairs and mahogany tables, it seemed too cold here, too sterile, and definitely too busy.

She missed Zed and Clarissa and Miss Bonita and...other parties. She hadn't spoken to Bael since he'd taken her statement about the murders. She knew it was the coward's way out to avoid him, she just knew that she wouldn't be able to leave town if she talked to him. She had to come back to the League offices, to revisit her life in D.C. She had to know if she could live with it or without it. This place had been her whole life before she arrived in Mystic Bayou, and now?

With all the phones ringing, elevators dinging and people bustling through the lobby shuffling through their files, Jillian was practically crawling out of her skin. She'd become far too accustomed to the quiet of her strange little house on the swamp. She'd taken a cab straight from the airport, not wanting to trap Sonja in the nightmare of a mid-day Dulles pick-up. Now she thought maybe she'd made a mistake, and that she should have stopped at home for a shower and a chance to steal Sonja's shoes.

Also, she thought maybe leaving without speaking to Bael was the wrong tactic to take. He hadn't even stopped by Miss Lottie's to say goodbye to her. What if he'd decided that she was too much trouble, what with her shadow government connections and serial killer abductions?

"SWEETIE!" she heard someone yell from across the lobby. She looked up to see Sonja running at full speed in four inch heels and a sapphire silk blouse and pencil skirt. Jillian stood just in time to practically be tackle-hugged by her friend, who was incredibly fleet of foot on her stilettos. "Oh my God, look at you. It's like you've spent the last couple of months at a spa. You're glowing."

"Well, I have been dealing with a lot of mud, I'll say that."

Sonja's almond shaped eyes tightened suspiciously. "No, seriously, you are really glowing, as in you're actually giving off a visible light. What is going on with you?"

"I just had a chance to relax for a bit, I guess."

"Naked? With that dragon guy?"

"A couple of times, yes, but we agreed not to see each other anymore. Because I live here and he lives in the middle of a swamp."

"Well, despite your slightly mopey tone, I hereby endorse this casual relationship. If anyone deserves some no-strings-attached sex, it's you."

"Thank you."

"Now, your meeting is scheduled for the east conference room. Please proceed to the door immediately. You don't want to keep the board waiting."

"Do they have all of the documents I sent ahead?" Jillian asked.

"Yes, beautifully collated and bound by yours truly."

"You're amazing."

"Knock 'em dead, sweetie." Sonja gave her a light shove in the direction of the conference room. "I'll put all of your bags in my office. Well, I'll have an intern do the carrying, but it still counts!"

Straightening her jacket collar, Jillian knocked softly on the conference room door. A feminine voice called for her to open the door. Jillian stopped in the doorway. She'd expected a table full of people, but only one seat at the table was occupied. And that seat was occupied by Akako Tomita. Jillian had never even made eye contact with Akako in the hallway. And here she was walking into a room alone with her.

Jillian shivered and rubbed her hands over her arms. She glanced down at the gooseflesh on her exposed wrist. That was weird.

Akako was wearing a deep scarlet suit and a necklace with nine points to represent the nine tails kept hidden while she was in her human form. She glanced up from a spiral bound document Jillian recognized as her report.

"Ms. Tomita? Am I early or late?" Jillian gestured toward the empty chairs.

Akako smiled coolly. "Neither. I wanted you to have my full attention for this meeting. The other board members tend to bring much confusion and noise with them, and I wanted you to know how much I appreciate the work you put into this publication. It is everything we hoped for and more."

She waited for the "but" that would inevitably follow such high praise. It didn't come.

"You should know that we expect big things from you, following such a performance. You've set the bar very high."

Jillian cleared her throat. "Thank you. Does this mean that the town will get the League resources they need?"

"Of course. I do have some questions, however."

There it was, the "but."

"You added the special appendix regarding the unexpected influences of the rift's energy on the town and how it's affecting the human citizens."

"Yes, I wasn't sure how much you would want the general public to know about that. It's going to be difficult enough to get humanity to accept the existence of so many *magique*. The idea that their kids, their neighbors, their dentist could turn into a *magie* because of some sort of interdimensional anomaly, that might be a little much."

"You are right there. For now, we're going to keep this chapter under our vest, but if it becomes necessary, we will publish it later."

"The scientist in me weeps, the person who doesn't want to see Mystic Bayou burn to the ground by an angry mob says thank you."

"And it seems to the board—and by the board, I mean myself because I speak for the board—this development requires further documentation."

"I agree. I have spoken to the local leadership about using League resources to investigate stabilizing the rift. They're interested. And frankly, I think that it's necessary to public safety to do so."

"It's good to know we're on the same page. How would you feel about working from Mystic Bayou for the foreseeable future?"

"What about the scheduled field work? With Dr. Montes out of commission—"

"Dr. Montes has been fired," Akako told her.

"While he's still in the hospital?"

"We cannot tolerate representatives of the League who will inappropriately touch interview subjects, no matter how much they contribute to their field."

Jillian wondered if that applied to Bael. Technically, she'd never officially interviewed him...so... She cleared her throat. "That seems like a reasonable requirement of employment. So, who's going to replace him?"

"We're composing a list of candidates. But in the meantime, we are going to need our top field representative in Mystic Bayou, where she has established strong community ties and a rapport with the key players. The other anthropologists can handle the lower priority field assignments."

"I would get to stay in Mystic Bayou?" Jillian's hand felt frozen around the conference table's edge. Was it possible she was hearing things? She would be able to go back home to the bayou. She could stay with Bael, if he agreed to speak to her again. She could stay with her friends, though Sonja was going to be pissed about Jillian leaving her alone in the apartment for the foreseeable future. Nothing could possibly turn out so perfect without a catch. Kitsunes were tricksters, after all. Would she owe Akako her firstborn child if she took this assignment?

"Absolutely. I'm a firm believer in not changing a situation that's working. Besides, you're going to need that time in the company of a tolerant blended community while you adjust to your new nature."

"I'm sorry?"

Akako suddenly sprung over the table, landing on the surface of the table in full *kitsune* form. Her face was set in feral lines, her jaw and nose shifting into a pointed snout. Her eyes were almond shaped and flaring with golden light. Nine nails bloomed behind her back, whipping back and forth with manic energy. She smiled, showing a mouthful of gleaming white fangs.

"Fuck!" Jillian knocked her chair back in her panic to make space between them. Also, she was on fire.

Jillian stared in horror at her own hand. Her whole body was engulfed in bright blue flames. She scrambled to her feet, her chair burning, sending billows of black smoke into Akako's face. The table was crackling under Akako's feet, buckling from the heat. Paperwork smoldered into ash and floated toward the ceiling.

Jillian beat at the flames on her chest, but it was too late. There wasn't a single part of her left untouched. She squeezed her eyes shut and waited for the burn to swallow her, to steal her breath and plunge her into pain.

But the only thing she sensed was the smoke alarm screaming to life.

She opened her eyes. She was still burning, surrounded in that blue light, but it didn't hurt. It barely tickled. It just felt right, like stretching muscles she'd held tense for too long. She raised her hands, watching the flames dance along her skin.

Akako was smiling softly at her, like she was staring at some long-admired precious piece of artwork.

The sprinkler system started spitting gallons of water on them both. And while it extinguished the table and the papers she'd burnt, her own blue flames were skill weaving and bobbing over her. She waved her fingers through it, but it was steadfast, consistently inconsistent.

"What is this?" Jillian demanded over the wail of the alarm.

"I want you to focus on drawing the fire back into you, like breathing air into your lungs. Don't panic. Don't try to force it. Just relax and breathe."

Jillian shook ever so slightly as she pictured the flames melting back into her skin, as naturally as the oxygen entering her lungs. Slowly, the blue fire died off and she flexed her fingers. She felt no pain, no burn, just the fizzing excitement of something new. Akako sat down in her chair, as if it was perfectly normal to continue a meeting with a sprinkler showering down over them.

"What was that?" she asked Akako.

"That was your inner fire. It's blue, which is interesting. A phoenix's flame usually reflects their emotional state. You must be very eager to return to the bayou, my dear."

"This is insane. I can't be a shapeshifter. I've never shown any signs of— Oh hell, the rift. When he took me that close to the rift, it must have changed me."

"You didn't notice that there was a difference?"

"I didn't feel any different. But now that you mention it, me being able to destroy Simon's dissection table with a jerk of my arms makes a lot more sense if I have super strength. Also, a few people have been looking at me differently because I've been glowing. I thought it was just the dragon sex."

Akako grinned. "Oh, really? Do tell. They were recognizing your new nature. We can sense each other, remember?"

Jillian remembered the sensation of her hair standing up on end when she walked into the room. "I thought I was just overwhelmed by industrial air-conditioning."

"Well, just be careful over the next few days and pick up a few extra fire extinguishers. And let me know when you've made a decision about the Mystic Bayou assignment."

"No—no I'll take it."

Akako grinned, her sharp fangs flashing. "Excellent news. I'm very pleased."

Jillian cleared her throat. "So, I have to ask, there were a lot of people in this office who you could've given this job. Why did you send me?"

"Dr. Ramsay, you may not know this but you have some support within the League's offices."

"Sure, Dr. Montes signed off on my dissertation. He helped me get the internship here."

"Actually, no, Dr. Montes was no help to you getting the internship at all."

Jillian frowned. "I'm...confused."

"You may not know this, but during World War II, my family was detained in an internment camp in California. It was difficult to be a minority during that time. It was even more difficult to be a minority within a minority. There was only one other shifter family at the camp, a family of kappas named Yamagita."

Jillian beamed. "You know Mel?"

"He was a child at the time but yes, we became very close friends. And when you went away to study, he was sure to call me and keep me updated on your progress. He had always been very proud of you. And when an internship became available, I arranged for Dr. Montes to check in on you at your college, to foster you along until you were ready for a position here."

"So I don't owe my job to a unicorn fondler? That's a relief."

Akako smirked. "Yes, well, please take a few days to enjoy your success and tie up any loose ends you need to secure before you leave town again. We look forward to your next report. I'll send you a list of deadline dates."

"Thank you."

Akako stood, shaking her hand. "Keep up the good work, Dr. Ramsay."

Stunned and a little shaky, Jillian walked out of the conference room. She'd just agreed to completely dismantle her life. And she'd set herself on fire. And she'd never been happier.

Sonja was standing in the hallway, a look of apprehension on her face. "Everything okay, sweetie? The fire alarm went off— Oh, holy hell, you're soaked to the skin. And your clothes are burned! What the hell happened in there? Did Akako Tomita attack you? I will cut that woman."

"She's a supernaturally strong ancient creature with nine blades hidden in her invisible tails."

"I would figure something out," Sonja insisted.

"She can also hear you." Jillian nodded toward the door. Sonja grimaced and they scurried down the hall to Sonja's office. Sonja shut the door behind them and started unpacking wet wipes, stain remover and a dry shirt from her emergency drawer.

"What happened?" Sonja demanded.

Jillian smiled sheepishly. "You're gonna be so mad at me."

18

BAEL

Bael walked into City Hall and everybody stopped talking. That was never a good sign. Even Gigi Grandent wouldn't make eye contact with him as he walked toward his office.

"Bael!" Zed yelled from his office. "I need you in here!"

Bael frowned, entering the room. "What's up?"

"So you gave Emily McAinsley a ticket."

"She was speeding."

"She was going three miles over the limit."

"Which is speeding!" Bael said, flopping into Zed's office chair.

"You made her cry! She's eighty-two years old. She was driving to the yarn store."

"She shouldn't be speeding! Honestly, she probably shouldn't be driving!"

"Ever since Jillian left, you've been an absolute bastard to everybody and it needs to stop now."

"This has nothing to do with Jillian."

"So, you're just making senior citizens cry for no reason?"

"I didn't mean to make her cry!" Bael leaned his head back on the chair. "Look, I realize I'm not... I'm struggling. I didn't know it was going to be this hard. Everything hurts. Everything seems gray. And the worst freaking part of it is there's no end in sight. She's not coming back and I didn't really give her much reason to. And I don't know what to do."

He looked up to see Zed holding out a tissue box, smirking at him. "Oh, fuck you, man!"

Zed burst out laughing. "Aw, come on, it's a little funny. You're finally expressing grown-up emotions. About a lady. It's completely uncharted territory."

"You're a dick."

"Look, I get it. You're miserable. But you can't make the rest of us miserable to keep it fair."

"I know." Bael pinched the bridge of his nose. "You're still a dick."

"Have you called her?"

"I don't want to interfere. She's gone back to her life. If she wanted to talk to me, she knows my number."

"Have you thought about going to see her in D.C.?"

Bael lifted his eyebrow. "How would that seem less desperate than calling her?"

"So I'm going to have to put up with miserable bastard Bael for, what? Another couple of decades?"

Bael nodded. "Conservatively, yes."

"Well, there's something to look forward to," Zed sighed. "So can you please go apologize to the octogenarian that you offended? And then go home and take a nap or roll around in your gold like Scrooge McDuck or whatever dragons do to calm their asses down?"

Bael's mind flashed back to Jillian's Scrooge McDuck joke, when they'd been naked and post-coital in his hoard. He shook his head and shoved the memory away. "I'll try."

"Thanks, now get the hell out of my office and don't make Gigi cry on the way out."

Bael grumbled. "Fine."

Bael walked back out of the lobby toward his car. He could go by the grocery and pick up some flowers to take to Emily, but that would probably be too much. He decided that a heartfelt apology was going to have to cut it. Because the woman had been speeding, dammit. He was only doing his job.

"Do you always walk around scowling like that?" he heard a familiar voice ask. "You know the League offers classes on how to be an effective and friendly public servant."

His head whipped toward the sound and suddenly the smell of flowers and books hit him with full force. Jillian was standing there, by his squad car. The sight of her face, her hair, every eyelash, was so familiar, and yet she'd changed. She was surrounded by this glow that seemed to shift between gold and blue.

Bael was vaguely aware that his mouth was hanging open, but he couldn't seem to close it. Or form words.

She frowned. "Or I have completely misread the situation and I should go."

Bael threw his arms around her and crushed her to his chest. "No."

She laughed, sliding her arms around him. He buried his nose in her hair. "Turns out my study's not done. The League liked my work so much that I'm going to write additional reports."

"So you're back? And you're staying?"

"I'll be staying here for a long time, maybe even permanently, which is handy, because I couldn't live anywhere else. I was miserable back in D.C., even though it was only a few days. I mean, I loved being able to see my friends, but it wasn't home anymore. No one was there to force feed me seafood when I was sad. No one was there to kidnap me and take me to parties when I was too wrapped up in work. And you weren't there." She wrapped her fingers around his left hand. "And I hated that you weren't there."

"Well, I was fine. Stalwart, manly stiff upper lip, and all that," he insisted.

"He's been a nightmare!" Zed yelled from the doorway. "An awful dick-ish nightmare."

Bael shrugged. "I might have been a little grumpy."

Jillian raised her brows. "Did Zed not tell you that I was coming back? The League called him two days ago to renew my lease on Miss Lottie's house."

Bael turned to Zed, his expression thunderously indignant. "*Couillon*! How could you?"

Zed jerked his massive shoulders. "More fun this way."

Jillian laughed. "That's pretty horrible, Zed."

"I was just so distraught from missing you, *catin*. I wasn't thinking straight."

Jillian pursed her lips. "I'll accept that."

"I was pretty much miserable, too," Bael admitted. "I'm awful glad you're back, because I would be very happy if you never left, ever again."

She nodded and he cupped her chin in his free hand and kissed her. He closed his eyes, leaning against the car. That nagging empty feeling haunting him over the last few weeks seemed to melt away and all he was left with was a feeling of contentment. And the smell of smoke.

No, the smoke was real. When he opened his eyes, he realized that he was engulfed by blue and gold flames. They were burning away his clothes, bubbling the paint of his squad car. And they were coming from Jillian.

"What in the hell?" he cried, jumping back. The flames seemed to slip back into Jillian's skin, leaving only the flames burning his clothes away.

Jillian winced and patted at his clothes. "Sorry, I forgot you're encased in polyester."

"What just happened?"

His shirt was pretty much a loss. Bael was just glad he'd decided to wear jeans this morning. Cotton burned slower than polyester. Otherwise, he might be standing on Main Street in his drawers.

"Yeah, a couple of things came up while I was gone," she said, snapping her fingers and smiling brightly as a blue three-inch flame grew out of her fingertip.

"I have feathers now," she said. "Also, my boss startled me and I turned into a purple and gold bird and set a conference table on fire."

"Well, that's new."

"As far as I can tell I got hit by some sort of wave energy from the rift when Simon dragged me out there. And it changed me, like it changed Ted and the others. So now I'm a shifter, too. My boss says I'm a phoenix."

He kissed her again. It made sense that his woman was a creature of rebirth and fire. She was the most doggedly persistent person he'd ever met. She never gave up, never stopped trying. Even when all indications were that it would be a really good idea to give up. He held her tight.

"Well, of course, you are. How could I expect anything less from the woman I love more than my own common sense?"

She tilted her head, squinting up at him. She brushed her fingers over his scalp. "You've never said you love me."

"Well, you've never said you loved me either. But I do, you're what I treasure most in the world and I was an idiot for letting you leave without telling you."

"I love you, too. I'm sorry I left. I just needed to be sure."

He kissed her again. "What about your life back home? What about Sonja and your coworkers?"

"Sonja is going to come visit. Fair warning, she's going to try to figure out whether you're good enough for me and inevitably conclude that you aren't. It's nothing personal. She's obligated by friendship to think no one deserves me. And I'll still be working with those coworkers, just from a distance. My life, as it is, is here with you."

He kissed her again, lazily, because they had all the time in the world now. "You know Miss Lottie's isn't exactly fireproofed, right?"

She nodded. "It had occurred to me."

"My place, however, is built to withstand dragonfire," Bael noted.

Jillian told him, "You're not nearly as subtle as you think you are."

"Wasn't trying to be subtle. I was just trying to get you home, into my den, as soon as possible."

"I think that can be arranged," she said, kissing him one last time. "But first, I have some questions for you."

His shoulders sagged. "You're kidding."

"You never let me interview you!"

"I told you things that I've never told anyone else!" Bael yelped.

"Until you fill out the questionnaire, it's not official. No questionnaire, no sex."

He shook his head. "That's so wrong."

She kissed him again and he closed his eyes, leaning into her. She murmured against his mouth. "I'll race you home."

"Wait, what?"

His eyes flew open just as a large purple and gold bird flew up from between his arms and rocketed up to the sky in a stream of blue flames.

Zed walked out of City Hall, staring at the trail of flames. "That'll take getting used to."

"Yep."

"You better catch her before she starts touching all your stuff."

Bael made a vaguely horrified face. "You don't think she'd do that, do you?"

Zed grinned. Bael took off running down the street, stripping out of his clothes. By the time he'd reached the pie shop, he'd shifted into a giant green and gold dragon and flew in the direction of his house.

LATER, after several of Bael's more vulnerable possessions had been burned to ash in their mad dash to the bedroom, two very tired *magique* lay curled on Bael's nest of pillows and blankets. Bael was dragging his fingers over her smooth skin, watching the golden light build beneath its surface.

Jillian sighed, leaning into the caress. "So, Simon was right. While I'm sure that there are benefits to *ahem*, absorbing dragon seed, my whole inner glow thing is more related to the rift changing me into a phoenix while I've lived here. A team of geneticists from the League are going to travel down here to ask the remade *magique* for DNA samples, to determine if there is some recessive gene that helps determine which humans transition."

Bael grumbled, even as he kissed the curve of her shoulder.

"They will ask very politely," she promised him.

"I'm not going to complain about the League bringing more people into town if it means you're staying."

She pushed him away, laughing. "You just growled when I talked about League scientists coming to town."

"Growling is not complaining."

"Well, knowing how secretive you dragons are, I will leave it to you and your family to decide how much you interact with the other League reps. I won't even tell them that we have dragons here in town. Though in retrospect, I really should have picked up on that quicker, given that there's a dragon on top of City Hall," she said.

"You had a lot on your mind," he said, holding her to his side. "And you were polite enough not to ask. And while we're talking about my family, I feel I should tell you that my grandfather was so disgusted by my mooning over a human girl—particularly after I refused his offer to arrange my marriage to a nice lady dragon from the old country—that he has officially decided to deny me my share of his hoard."

"So I'm going to have to settle for a man who can only provide me with a treasure that fills an industrial sized warehouse?" she scoffed. "I think between that and my salary, we can make ends meet."

"This is serious dragon stuff, sweetheart. I need to know that you're really comfortable with it."

"I am, I promise. But that reminds me." She paused to lace their fingers together. "You never told me your dragon name."

"Well, I wasn't sure you were going to stay. You made it pretty clear that you planned on going back to D.C. Besides, I've never told anyone my true dragon name. Not even Zed."

"You showed me your hoard!"

"Well, a dragon name is different. It's something that's only shared between children and parents, between mates. It gives the bearer power over the dragon. You can force me to give you part of my hoard. You can force me out of my dragon form and make me human again. That's why you don't see a lot of dragon divorces."

"I would never do that!" she exclaimed. "That's awful. What's the point in having a dragon name in the first place if it's just going to be used to hurt you?"

"It's a sign of trust. And it gives you the best kind of power over me, more than you already have, anyway. For instance, if you call my true name, I have to answer and I would hear it anywhere. So, if you're ever in trouble, you can summon me to you."

She bolted up, mouth agape as she stared down at him. "That would have been really helpful to know a couple of weeks ago. You know, when I was kidnapped by a serial killer."

"Well, I didn't know you were going to be kidnapped by a serial killer!"

Jillian grumbled, "Likely story."

"It's probably not going to happen again."

"Well, I would hope not," she snorted.

Bael sat up, still holding her hands, and took a deep breath. "My dragon name is...Dave."

"What?"

He shrugged. "Most dragon parents give their offspring names like Qytharn the Bold or Cyveriaus the Silent Dread, because they think it will make them grow up strong and scary. No one would ever guess that my secret dragon name is Dave."

She nodded. "It frightens me how much that makes sense."

"I need your solemn promise that you will not use the name 'Dave' in any way unless it is an absolute emergency," he said, touching his forehead to hers. "Or in the throes of ecstasy, because there are some interesting side benefits there, too."

She nodded and kissed him. "I promise. I will not call you 'Dave,' unless it's absolutely necessary."

"Thank you." He kissed her and a beautiful light warmth spread from her chest through to her toes. He wrapped his arms around her and they burrowed deeper into their nest.

"Do phoenixes have true names?" she asked, nestling her head against his throat. "Like if I decide to go really exotic and call myself 'Debbie,' will that give you some supernatural power over me?"

"You'd have to ask Earl. But please pick something other than Debbie. I dated a Debbie in high school and she was horrible." He shivered under her.

"Make me a list of your horrible ex-girlfriends and I'll choose something else. This is a very strange conversation."

"Well, none of our conversations have ever been what you'd call ordinary."

She chuckled. "We need to find a girl for Zed."

"I don't think there's a girl alive who could put up with Zed."

"It would get Clarissa off of his back."

He rolled over her, hitching her legs over his hips. "I don't want to talk about Zed right now."

"Fair enough...Dave."

THE END

DISCOVER MORE BY MOLLY HARPER

****all lists are in reading order****

The Southern Eclectic Series (contemporary women's fiction)
Save a Truck, Ride a Redneck (prequel novella)
Sweet Tea and Sympathy
Peachy Flippin' Keen (novella)
Ain't She a Peach?

The Mystic Bayou Series (paranormal romance)
How to Date Your Dragon
Love and Other Wild Things – coming in 2019

The "Sorcery and Society" Series (young adult fantasy)
Changeling
Fledgling – coming in 2019

The "Nice Girls" Series (paranormal romance)

Nice Girls Don't Have Fangs
Nice Girls Don't Date Dead Men
Nice Girls Don't Live Forever
Nice Girls Don't Bite Their Neighbors

Half-Moon Hollow Series (paranormal romance)
The Care and Feeding of Stray Vampires
Driving Mr. Dead
Undead Sublet (A story in The Undead in My Bed anthology)
A Witch's Handbook of Kisses and Curses
I'm Dreaming of an Undead Christmas
The Dangers of Dating a Rebound Vampire
The Single Undead Moms Club
Fangs for the Memories
Where the Wild Things Bite
Big Vamp on Campus
Accidental Sire

The "Naked Werewolf" Series (paranormal romance)
How to Flirt with a Naked Werewolf
The Art of Seducing a Naked Werewolf
How to Run with a Naked Werewolf

The "Bluegrass" Series (contemporary romance)
My Bluegrass Baby
Rhythm and Bluegrass
Snow Falling on Bluegrass

Standalone Titles
And One Last Thing
Better Homes and Hauntings

ABOUT THE AUTHOR

Molly Harper worked for six years as a reporter and humor columnist for The Paducah Sun. Her reporting duties included covering courts, school board meetings, quilt shows, and once, the arrest of a Florida man who faked his suicide by shark attack and spent the next few months tossing pies at a local pizzeria.

She has published over 30 books. She writes women's fiction, paranormal romance, romantic comedies, and young adult fantasy.

Please visit her website for updates, news and freebies! https://www.mollyharper.com/

facebook.com/Molly-Harper-Author-138734162865557

twitter.com/mollyharperauth

instagram.com/mollyharperauthor

CPSIA information can be obtained
at www.ICGtesting.com
Printed in the USA
LVHW030252250220
648116LV00002B/337